American Foreign Policy

American Foreign Policy

A Novel

JOHN ZEUGNER

RESOURCE *Publications* · Eugene, Oregon

AMERICAN FOREIGN POLICY
A Novel

Resource Publications
An Imprint of Wipf and Stock Publishers
199 W. 8th Ave., Suite 3
Eugene, OR 97401

www.wipfandstock.com

PAPERBACK ISBN: 978-1-6667-3019-7
HARDCOVER ISBN: 978-1-6667-2136-2
EBOOK ISBN: 978-1-6667-2137-9

03/18/22

719

The South Wind—has a pathos
Of individual Voice—
As One detect on Landings
An Emigrant's address.

A Hint of Ports and Peoples—
And much not understood—
The fairer—for the farness—
And for the foreignhood.
　　　—EMILY DICKINSON, 1863

Draft Manuscript

by Thomas Ausa

Contents

Part I

The Open Door and the Closed Heart

Chapter One

Creighton's understanding of the senselessness of what he was doing began at the halfway point of a "Cruise Through Exotic Southeast Asia," and culminated a year later in Professor Sears' Strategy Seminar. A colleague at Creuset Catholic College (known as "CCC" by Creighton's elderly fellow faculty) had warned him: "Of course a cruise is always tonic, but it may be an inadequate distraction for the really tough change you've experienced. You're right to seek distraction, but it may not be adequate for the trauma you've endured." At the time Creighton wondered if the collapse of his marriage and the estrangement from his tiny daughter qualified as "trauma". But it had occurred at the end of the spring semester and providentially there was a final reduction on a single cruise ticket that coincided with a special "professional development grant for contingent faculty" made available by the administration in return for an end to discussion of unionization. Beyond that administrative appeasement, or perhaps embarrassment, Creighton sensed his department chair, a fellow Creighton actually liked and respected, had pushed through the development grant for Creighton as a kind of consolation prize for losing the underpinnings of his life—marriage, family, and contingent near gig work. Apparently no one wanted to dispute whether a cruise counted as professional development. So Creighton filed his grades, flew to Seattle, and departed on the Empress of the East.

The cruise underscored his dissolution and dizziness. In Kuala Lumpur he internalized the rich green cricket pitch surrounded by mosques that were encircled yet by gleaming glass hotel and office towers—. How could such circles co-exist since each was a profound distraction to the others? Distraction began to dominate his thinking, his justification for taking the cruise itself. In KL he began to realize that distraction as a way of life, left him entirely leftover, aimless, and untracked—so much so that he no longer understood the meaning of the word "aimless". It seemed he'd stepped into an abyss where the most committed moment of his tenure in that chasm centered around finding bacon for breakfast in the Muslim citadel of dietary denial.

He was sick during the stopover at Singapore; a mangling near dysentery kept him aboard ship for the two days. Or was it the fear some authorities on the land might know he had been chewing cannabis gum and carelessly dropping a paper wrapping cascade of damning evidence. So they'd have to condemn and convict him to a bamboo and razor wire jail for the rest of his brief life. But the true abyss opened in the next stop, Phnom Penh, Cambodia.

Upon docking the Empress was confronted with a phalanx of white coated Cambodians who insisted no foreigner aboard ship could depart until passing a rigorous interrogation, and tests for Covid 19. Creighton showed his vaccination card and did not mention recent dysentery and was cleared for a bus to Siam Reap, one of the peak attractions of the cruise. A gleaming, white bus was waiting at the sea wall beyond the docks. A short man was waving a cruise flag and beckoning the passengers. Creighton was winded when he got to the bus and quickly took the seat behind the driver. The air conditioning was on full blast and Creighton felt the chill acutely. He felt woozy again and his stomach seemed roiling mildly with a threat of sudden evacuation; he tightened and endured the four hours of lumpy, lurching passage, allegedly, to another spiritual realm that turned out to be a muddy extensive parking lot surrounded by what appeared to be live oak trees. The fellow with the red flag led the stunned busmates slowly out of the lot to a line of port-o-lets and then down a wide dirt path to a mammoth corner of an immense temple or shrine that looked, Creighton thought, like a stone textile mill he'd seen in New Hampshire. Soon enough the mill analogy diminished as the wall sprung alive with chiseled figures in flight, in sexual congress, in daily farming tasks. Gradually the stones grew larger, majestically so, and the full amazing panoply of Ankor Wat scored with green moss stretched beyond his view. At length the bus tour line came to a massive fresh wooden construction of some eighty steps, set at an angle that seemed almost 65 degrees. The wooden steps were at least thirty feet long and there were no railings anywhere in sight. To reach the Wat's entrance you'd have to climb the steps.

For an anguished moment Creighton wondered if the steps hadn't been borrowed from a Cambodian bootcamp obstacle course. He sat on a flat stone opposite the steps, and, just as several of his bus mates, chattering fiercely, began their ascent, he felt his legs go dead, inert, paralyzed in his nifty Dr. Marten boots purchased for the trip. How could the monks rely on a wooden structure to bring tourists to the most massive stone edifice in Asia? Didn't they understand the absurdity of such a juxtaposition? Of course, they didn't, and all he could do about it, was slowly sob at their idiocy, and his own, for imagining a cruise could shut out the abyss he saw beneath his feet. Tears washed down his cheeks and his hands rammed into the edge of the stone to keep him from falling into the endless falling-away courting him in the trough beside the temple. A couple of his elderly bus-mates came to stand beside him, also dubious that they could make the climb. Others midway up were reduced to hunching over on all fours to make it atop the last thirty-five steps, each taken in a panting, slow-motion scramble.

"I can't do it," Creighton said to anyone listening. "I can't do it. Too steep. I haven't the strength. I haven't. I'll go back to the bus."

"Of course you will. We'll go with you, if you want."

"That won't be necessary, I think. I'll get my legs moving again soon."

"Not now?"

"No. Not now. Maybe in a little while. I need to rest." Creighton wiped his sleeve on his cheek. "Not now." He wondered how he could have imagined a cruise would be distraction enough from the disaster of his collapsing life. How could it ever possibly have been distraction enough?

Now looking at the enormous. incongruous wooden steps to the massive stone edifice he felt exactly as he did upon opening the trunk of his Honda Civic after any class— before the commuting run to the next class at the next college or university. Emptiness and futility. He'd toss his scarred bookbag into the boxes of ungraded exams or binders full of aging class notes, sometimes specific lectures, set off with colored inserts. How many minutes to the next show, how many miles to the next appearance and identical sense of absurdity? They'd given him the cruise as a kind of consolation prize for bankruptcy in every aspect—from economic circumstance to simple self-regard. He was a shadow presence in three campuses, unrecognized, beyond his three pasted seals of parking permission. "Oh, I see now, you're an adjunct and that's why I don't know you at all," a colleague had remarked almost identically at each venue.

Once when despair reached full surge, he created a card that read:

> "Hi There! I'm a contingent faculty member. Wouldn't you like to learn my name? After all, your light teaching load, your raise, your released time, your large single office, your sabbatical, your benefits, and your job security are enabled by your exploitation of me . . . Maybe that's why my name is *anathema?*"

Printing the card was too expensive, so he repeated the paragraph four times on a single sheet and contemplated scissoring the sentiment for distribution but gave up the ghost.

Ah yes, the road warrior. The scholar on wheels, teacher on the skateboard, skittering from one course here, one course there, until enough courses equaled something less than a living wage. And always fueled by the seduction of performance before potentially enthusiastic audiences. Young minds open to seduction, and of course the tantalizing hope of tenure someday, a permanent position with benefits and health insurance. A shot at the ladder from adjunct rung to visitor step, to post-doc position, to professor of practice, to full time something other than tenured faculty, lately something like "teaching professor" or "full time lecturer" or "staff"—anything that signaled something beyond fingernails gripping the edge of teaching abyss's lip— all made of mica. And he heard, just before uneasy sleep, crackling, crumbling sounds and watched bloody flakes in his fingertips.

And now before what he had traveled around the planet to see, now before what they had given him as reward for endless self-abasement, now before one of humankind's most noble creations—an edifice made against all local supplies, of inspiration-demanding stones quarried and dragged from hundreds of miles away, before this very temple of the noblest, sanest, most deeply peaceful assertions of humanity's greatest aspiration, now before this marvel at last he had been struck dumb inert, useless, impotent, a perfect glop of a being unable to waddle to the steps much less ascend them, a legless, armless, gutless fool who realized he had surrendered his whole life to idiot distractions believing them to give him breath when in fact he was choking to death.

Here, dumped before the greatest imaginable distraction he suddenly perceived distraction itself sucked, yes sucked you dry of all care, connection, possibility. Yes, he knew suddenly that distraction itself was the stalest of all ornaments, the frailest of all calls on his stupid life.

"Do you need help standing up?"

"I'm afraid so. My legs have gone numb. I'm so sorry."

"No need to be sorry. Tiffany and I will brace you walking. We're tough folks."

Tough Folks?? Tough Folks? Tiffany and I, tough folks? Indeed, tough folks. Beefy arms around him. Dragging him forward, back toward the bus as if he were a rag doll. And on that long drag scuffing route he realized something magical. There was a way out of perfect distraction, a way through the maze, a way to break the overhead ice and get shut of the annihilating chill. Yes, there was a path beyond the stars, a lilting galloping sparkling steed just clamoring for him to hop on. The great horse Atrocity was the path to Elysium. He needed to find the supreme act of atrocity, the most heinous crime he could imagine, could fashion, could conjure out his purest desperation—an act so horrendous, so tainted with hideousness with unimaginable horror that simply accomplishing it would release him from his softly pliable infinite cage of despair.

He was buoyed beyond any suppression now, even though he did not know the act yet that would free him. He felt that the dragging scuffling was but prelude to vaulting escape. He had only to turn up the volcano of butchery to realize deliverance. And soon enough he sensed he could do that almost effortlessly and completely. The finest atrocity would make him whole.

Chapter Two

In Georgetown's failing sunlight there were several ways to think about noise: intrusion; distraction, substitution; relief. And today's seminar speaker was making an appropriate point about noise shrouding out message in the world of intelligence even as an enormous, navy-blue garbage truck picked up the scarred green Dempsey Dumpster immediately beyond the colonial windows of the Strategy Institute's first floor seminar room. The dumpster rose obliquely in the window, and, as the truck throttled up, grinding toward emptying, the seminar speaker fastened on the words "nuggets amidst noise," as the central tenet of his argument. Something about real Soviet intentions in the Middle East versus the noise of Soviet rhetoric at the UN or Geneva or Bayonne—Perth Amboy perhaps. That, thought Creighton, would make a good question: "You said Beirut, but didn't you really mean Bayonne? The sounds are similar, similar noise, aren't they?"

Upended rubbish clattered through Creighton's imagined jokes. And instead of mockery he suddenly heard a clear, amazingly sharp plinking sound, the resonant skittering in slowed time of a large, triangular shaped rock down the dirt-dappled, shining children's slide in the park across from the Institute. At the top of the slide was the little girl's smiling face, her left cheek smudged with hot cocoa stain, a face stunningly joyous as the rock clipped down toward Creighton's daughter Jenna. He relived his stupefying paralysis at the plinking, plinking downward rushing danger to his two-year-old girl. Frozen as the rock flailed across the polished aluminum, firing nicks on the descent. And above the threat, the incredible squeals of the girl who had tossed the stone—wondrous squeals of anticipated hurt. Jenna seemed unable to move—so, the three of them: one screaming deliriously on high; Creighton helpless by the steps to the top of the slide, and Jenna standing at the slide's bottom edge directly in the path of the sharp stone. The three of them cemented in a tableau amid discussion of noise and compacting trash. The truck's compressor was overwhelming. The windows shook. Bone china coffee cups rattled on the gleaming oak seminar table. "I am talking now of deception of the highest kind, conscious, deliberate, conspiratorial, a veritable campaign of delusion—disinformation at every interval. I am talking about covert delivery of missiles never introduced in the region, even as pious peace declarations are deliberately made in every embassy concerned. I am talking about a torrent of deception such as cannot be imagined, except by those clearly knowledgeable about the wiles instinctively followed by totalitarian regimes. I am talking about a monstrous—"

The stone missed Jenna, but Creighton replayed the near-miss endlessly. Should he have pushed the slide over? Just punishment for the strange little girl who tossed the rock. Would that action have deflected the stone, saved Jenna, who, it turned out, needed no saving anyway? The rock skittered beyond her, came to pleasant rest on the dusty cold dirt at the benches set up for thoughtful, caring parents to watch their happy offspring.

"Jesus Christ, Sybil!" The woman on the bench shouted above all the traffic noise. "Jesus Christ! You get down here now! You coulda killed her. You wanted too, didn't ya? Didn't ya? Jesus Christ! You get down here." The woman came charging off the bench with a frenzy Creighton decided later perfectly matched Sybil's squeals of joy. And clearly Sybil (could a child be so named?) was terrified by this parental stone clamoring up the slide. The girl jumped right at Creighton in haste to retreat before the avenging mother.

"Don't you dare run away, you little brat! Don't you move a fucking muscle!"

Creighton tightened motionless as the girl also froze at his side. But capitulation was not apparently enough for the woman sputtering worse came at them. In a wide swift arc she swung an odd, polished maroon vinyl handbag at Sybil's head. The girl never ducked, but took the blow that bounced her off Creighton's leg and then into the dirt.

"Sorry, mister," the woman said. "Now you get up, you little brat and you apologize. You hear me?"

"It's okay. It's okay." Creighton heard himself say, indeed, plead. "Nobody got hurt. Jenna's okay. Nobody got hurt." Except Sybil of course.

"You apologize. You do it!" The woman didn't hear Creighton, so he picked the little girl up, shielded her. Her eyes were glazed, indifferent perhaps stunned, he couldn't tell. Red welt on her stained cheek.

"You try and ya try," the woman said slowly, as if savoring the words. "Ya try and ya try. For What? So, she's trying to kill somebody. God! What's the fucking use?"

The obscenity Creighton decided was a second stone coming down the slide. He imagined Jenna would be pestering him about the word's meaning all the way back to the hotel.

"Nobody got hurt. No need for an apology. It was an accident."

The woman laughed. "She's the accident," the woman said. "I'm the accident. You're an accident. Everything's a fucking accident."

"There's no need to swear. My daughter doesn't hear words like that," Creighton said with self-surprising evenhandedness.

The woman looked at him with widening eyes. His little stone then?

"Yeah, yeah, you're right of course. Of course you're right. I'm really sorry. Her father used to rag on me for my mouth. Maybe that's why he split."

"Maybe so," Creighton was surprised to hear himself say.

The woman looked at him, then smiled a slow, disorganized grin, as if she were trying to find humor in his remark. "Yeah, well I wouldn't want to offend your little girl." The woman emphasized 'offend' then moved back to the bench.

"In the third phase of negotiation breakdown," the seminar speaker was saying in an oddly accented, agitated way, "all sides retreat into hardened positions, becoming separate bureaus of noise, unable to hear any other position. The structure becomes ever more cacophonous. And resolution if it comes at all, comes from outside. Must be imposed. Must be legislated by others beyond the legitimizing process of the negotiation. That seldom happens but even if it does occur, we have problems of implementation—really negation of implementation that needs to be organized, named, categorized, and understood. So, let's get started in those tasks; we have the time this afternoon to lay out a full listing . . ."

The giant blue garbage truck would not be back for two days, Creighton thought, and by then the room would either be empty or perhaps filled with an entirely different set of strategy analysts.

2.

Because the contract stipulated that Creighton's ex-wife got custody of Jenna including every Christmas, Creighton got Jenna for each Thanksgiving. But the strategy seminar in Washington coincided with the holiday. Creighton might have proposed a swap, or he might have cancelled her coming, but the contract was still relatively new and not subject, now at least, to revision. And cancellation would only have verified the implication of indifference that had led to the contract. So he decided to bring Jenna to the Ramada Inn on N Street just off Logan Circle, to a tidy, spacious efficiency unit. He hired Holly, a grad student from George Washington University to watch Jenna in the afternoons. Mornings he took Jenna to the little park. She liked the slide and she liked, she said, meeting Sybil.

"Sure. Why not?" the woman explained, "all two-year-olds like risks and playing with Sybil is taking a big risk, putting your life right on the line. She's not interested in the sound the rock makes. She wants to watch it skip right down into somebody's eye. She really does! I know what she's thinking. She's thinking a little pain makes things more interesting. Ya get it?"

Creighton wondered if a reply were needed.

"Do ya?"

"Pain?"

"Yeah, pain. P. A. I. N. Get it?" The woman laughed, a raucous, phlegmy, harsh laugh. She slumped down on the bench. Her legs pushed out further, heels of loafers digging into the grey dirt. "I got a lot of pain, but these keep it, keep it way under control." The woman brought out a small plastic bottle from her green, quilted coat. "How come you got so much time in the morning? Ya laid off?"

"No. I work . . . I work in the afternoons and evenings."

"Late shift?"

"Yes."

"I don't think so, but ya know something? I don't care. I really don't care. Really. Really." She stretched the word out. "Sybil doesn't either." The woman laughed. "We just come here when we like. Whenever."

"They seem to play together pretty well."

"Sybil's just setting her up before she tries to kill her."

Creighton laughed. The woman opened her plastic bottle and took one more yellowish pill.

"Fifteen dollars a pop on 14thStreet," the woman said, "But I get 'em for $11.50 per 15, because I 'need' them. Medically that is."

"What are they?"

"Oh, aren't we interested all of a sudden? Percodan. Percodan to get things started. Quaaludes to keep things finished nicely and the frayed edges trimmed off. That's how we used to talk, didn't we? Oh, you are interested!"

Sybil had picked up Jenna, carrying her under the arms. In flopping unison they walked- waddled toward the swings about twenty feet from the slide. Creighton's breath condensed in the air. The grey dull sky portended snow. He watched Sybil arrange Jenna on a swing. She gave one anxious glance in his direction. Perhaps a plea for intervention?

The woman put a yellow capsule into Creighton's hand. "You try it. Helps a lot."

"I'm not interested."

"You're interested all right, but if you don't want it, give it back."

"I'll keep it for a rainy day."

"Heh, heh," the woman said.

"I'll bet your name is Claire," Creighton said.

The woman smiled. "Who was Claire?"

"Was is the right word."

"I know. I know. She got run over by a snowplow in Cleveland." The woman said, pursing her lips apparently to fight down a smile.

"Precisely. Sheared off her left shoulder and most of her left forehead." Creighton answered. "Tossed her back against some storage sheds where that night attack-Dobermans ate her."

"You and Sybil!" the woman laughed, "You and Sybil!"

Jenna had been seated on the rounded old wooden board of the swing and slowly Sybil was winding her up, spinning her so the chains formed a single strand. When the chains were sufficiently tightened above Jenna's head, Sybil turned the board loose. Jenna started a slow spin, then gathered momentum.

Once again the seminar speaker intersected Creighton's shuddering remembrances. "Why introduce such weapons into the region? Weapons whose sole function was offensive, whose presence was guaranteed to change the equation of power in ways that might not be, surely would not be predictable or manageable. And yet doing this while hiding it all under the cloak of 'equivalency restoration'? And doing so, too, under the fantastic smoke screen of pious peace pretentions!"

Jenna in the escalating twirl reached up an arm, evidently to grab the chain. To stop the spinning? Or just delight in the unraveling torque? Who could say? Each turn took her tiny hand away from the source of the twirl. She kept reaching back in. And the twist was finally undone. The strands momentarily separated, Jenna's hand on the right chain. But momentum carried the chains back together. Sybil added her force to the spinning board. Of course, the chains would rewrap, this time in the opposite direction. Of course, Creighton thought, paralyzed again as Jenna's hand, forearm disappeared into the swirling tangle. Then her agonized shrieking catapulted him from the bench. Sybil kept spinning the seat, tightening the linkage around Jenna's arm. The links popped into Jenna's flesh. Blood burst out. Creighton imagined he saw tendons snap. And her cries carried over the traffic, over the innocent and contented passing cars beyond the Institute, carried beyond the clever syncopation of Creighton's recognition of the speaker's harsh verdict on Soviet duplicity, carried beyond the remembered and now longed-for distracting dumpster pickup truck.

Creighton drew out a wide, white handkerchief (he only carried them during Jenna's visits). Holding this white flag he sprawled at the low swing, fell at the edge of the swing, but managed to stop the spinning. Sybil shrieked angrily, kicked at him, tried to shove the seat further into its cycle of re-entrapment. Would the little forearm snap in two? Creighton got to his knees. The mud felt cold on his kneecaps. He yanked the seat motionless. Jenna had stopped screaming. Her face had gone white. Her eyes gotten gigantic with stun. Blood gushed down her head. Creighton couldn't tell which way to spin the swing. Then Jenna made a soft, mewling sound. Was she saying, "Daddy? Mommy?" Sybil belted Creighton across the face with what felt like a stone in her left hand. He shoved her away, only bringing on heightened screaming and then Sybil was sprinting off toward the traffic. The woman, maroon vinyl bag flailing, sprinted after Sybil.

Which way to unwind? Hands off the edge of the seat. Of course, the chains would naturally unravel, naturally seek separation. How much flesh gobs would come with them?

Again, the strategy speaker intruded: "This administration's policy has been to pretend otherwise, quite otherwise, but what an effort it requires! How much attention to detail! Plug every opening; fill in information gashes in the silly fabric of self-deception . . ."

3.

The two resident physicians at the Emergency Room of George Washington University Hospital were burly, bushy-faced, and improbable saviors. And barely competent Creighton guessed. The large one kept brushing at the left side of his mustache, as Jenna's blood soaked through the towel the taxi driver had loaned Creighton. Were there snapped tendons? No one but the surgeon "on his way down" could say. Only Sybil in the soft, rose light of the waiting area looked radiant, beatific. She rocked happily on her mother's lap while Creighton fingered another proffered yellow capsule. In the taxi coming back to the hotel he finally took it. Tendons were intact. A mere nine stitches required, and some codeine for the "severe discomfort."

"Ya didn't get her yet, Sybil," the woman said, "but ya got more chances, don't ya?"

They all went back to the Ramada Inn. Sybil turned on the T.V., lay down on the chocolate carpeting. Jenna fell asleep on the queen size bed. Creighton was afraid to move her to the crib he had rented. For one thing, the bars didn't lower, and the reach over the rungs bothered him. For another his arms felt like cement, legs like soft paste. The silly gold cranes in the wallpaper turned to watch them. Creighton and the woman sat at the hexagonal Formica dining table.

"Funny they wouldn't let you pay," she said.

"Hmmn," Creighton answered smiling.

"Nice, eh?" the woman said.

"Nice," Creighton answered.

"Look, I got this great hash. Opiated. Two tokes and 'whee cried Bobby!' Get it?"

"Hmmn," Creighton said.

"So you want some?"

"Whee cried Bobby!"

"The woman laughed.

"I'm missing my seminar." Creighton said sappily.

"Seminar," the woman repeated the word, apparently musing on it. "Seminar . . . sem eh nar . . ." she laughed.

She seemed about to say it again, but Creighton cut her off. "What is your name?"

After a moment she said, "You know it. You said it already."

"You're actually Claire?"

She didn't answer, instead took out an anchovy-shaped, poorly rolled cigarette and lit it. In long double intake she clamped her mouth and rolled her eyes a bit before slowly releasing the smoke from her lungs. "Yes, Claire, and you knew it instinctively, didn't you?"

"It's a name I knew."

"Actually, it's Bonnie. I'm not the Claire of your dreams."

"Neither was Claire."

"Better take a toke. It'll help."

Creighton took a long drag, held it unconscionably long and then watched its creepy dispersing from his nose and mouth. He passed it back while taking a further inhalation

19

of the residue cloud. "They're sleeping and I envy them," Creighton said.

"I'm gonna draw a bath," she said and got up heading toward the bathroom.

"Jenna's the one who needs a bath."

"Who'd you think I'm drawing it for? Ah, ya thought it was for us. That's sweet. But it's for them. Here's what I propose. I draw the bath and we drown both of them in it."

"Great idea. Gets rid of our troubles. Cheaper than day care." Creighton answered.

She laughed and continued, "Exactly—no more sharing, no more diapers, no more whining. Done and finished. We're finally freed up. They'll think it's fun till we hold them under." She said from the bathroom.

4.

"The essence of diplomacy is to unyoke fear, to take away the dread of mutual annihilation, to stop the speed of breathing and to release imagination, so as to free the finding of solutions. To get shut of choking and suffocation and sample the liberation inherent in alternatives recognized and suddenly embraced as if discovered in a cave speared suddenly by sunlight. When it's done right, it's intoxicating. I'm not just sounding jejune. I mean it's really intoxicating. It puts you to flailing about in ways no one has ever experienced— knitting together what hitherto was inert at the bottom of deadest, stalest sea."

Listening Creighton longed for the garbage truck for he remembered in its emptying watching a translucent very tough plastic bag bulging with something flesh colored, small arm-like and streaming hair stretched across the vinyl—dark, wondrously thin tinsel. A pair of small heads with upturned eyes and strange, red mucus streaming from their smudged noses. It seemed they were straining at the translucent containment, punching the vinyl outward as black bags tumbled from the dumpster into the compressing chamber of the truck's hydraulically sliding belly.

Pressing downward Bonnie had shouted with mounting joy, "No more nappies. No more whining. No more shitty negotiating over dinner! And why, for God's sake, are you holding up her arm? Surely not to save sutures. Not that! You tender asshole! Jesus! You kill me. You actually want to preserve the stitching rather than life itself. What a screwed-up bastard you are!"

Why, Creighton recalled, was the bathroom so infernally hot? How did its mucidness thicken like a swaddling electric blanket cranked beyond its highest setting? And why was there such thrashing, churning, screaming water slosh cascading up at him?

"We need to get so far beyond comparing throw weights or matching nautical miles. We have to recognize the mirror images in our negotiating, in our mutual rhetoric, in our studied dissections of each initiative, bracketing everything with sorrowful resignation. Our surrenders to worst case analysis, and mutual trampling of inherent bad faith models in our collective brains. But perhaps even the boldest, most brilliant diplomacy cannot shed so much dead skin. Do you think?" And there was a pause that extended into silence tightening from the table. "What do you think?" the speaker asked again. When no spoke, he turned and directly asked Creighton, "What do you think? Have I made a naïve case? What do think? What do you think?"

Creighton answered, "It sounds so . . . so very, very hollow."

Chapter Three

When the seminar ended, the speaker motioned to Creighton to come to the podium. The gesture didn't seem threatening, almost comradely, and Creighton responded with an unanticipated happiness that led him to open with an apology.

"Professor Sears, I certainly meant no disrespect in using the word 'hollow.'"

"No. No. I felt none. In fact I thought the word had a persuasive strangeness to it. Strangely apt. Apt in that I agree with you, after a while the whole rhetoric of Grand Strategy has a kind of empty hollowness to it. A kind of logical construct that politicians like Gorbachev and Reagan could very pleasingly cut through to reach . . . to reach almost obvious conclusions. But obvious only after they announced them. Yes. Yes. Strangely apt."

"Strangely apt," Creighton repeated. "I'm afraid I'm not up to normal discourse right now. I lost my two-year daughter yesterday to a grotesque accident."

"My God," Sears said, "I'm so sorry. Of course language fails at such a time."

"It does . . . so it does," Creighton said. "Strangely apt maybe catches it. Does it?" There was a question for Sears to ponder, Creighton thought, while I ponder how to fill in the *grotesque accident.*

"My God. I'm so sorry for your loss. How did it happen?"

Creighton paused looked away, then turned away, drawing a long, apprehendable breath. In the pause Creighton felt a certain heart-felt concern emanating from Sears, and Creighton stretched out the interval creating, he believed, a certitude to the experience of tragedy. He wanted to let Sears marinate in that fellow feeling, softening him up for the lack of detail Creighton rummaged around in his head attendant to the mythical accident. There was nothing accidental in Jenna's clawing at his forearm as he forced her head below the myriad bubble laden warm waters. When the pause grew long enough for comment, Creighton in a choked voice said softly, "Sorry. I'm sorry . . ."

Sears immediately added, "No need. It was thoughtless of me to ask specifics. I can only imagine what you're going through."

"Hollow, so very hollow," Creighton said rasping.

"Of course. Of course."

Interiorly a solemn voice in Creighton's mind toyed with the declaration that it didn't actually happen. Jenna would be waiting for him by the bottom of the slide, arm intact, silly, incessant laughter radiating like glinting sparks in rescued consciousness. Creighton found himself asking Sears, "Could you grant me absolution?"

"What?"

Creighton realized he'd asked for something beyond strategic thinking. He beat a hasty retreat, "For using the word hollow so callously. I need your forgiveness."

"Don't be ridiculous. Absolutely no need. Good policy demands sharp interrogation, even rudeness to drive out irrelevancy or faulty premises."

"Faulty premises," Creighton repeated slowly. "For example, the notion that life has a regularity to it, a series of predictable occurrences with normality to them, an expected litany of successes like birthdays. Maybe exactly like empty birthdays."

Sears nodding added, "Perhaps . . ."

"Empty birthdays. That's what I'll face." Creighton thought such personal reflection ought to end all attempted inquiry and was delighted to see that it did so.

Abruptly Sears said, "Look. I'm so sorry for your loss, but, and I'm embarrassed to say it, I have grad students waiting with bated breath for my tutorial to start. I've got to be going. But please email me if you need anything. Please keep in touch." He patted Creighton's shoulder, turned and headed swiftly toward the narrow corridor away from the auditorium's right entrance, but paused to listen to Creighton's declaration.

"Justice is the interest of the stronger, isn't it? Isn't that so? The interest of the stronger who can easily drown a two-year old. Isn't that so?"

Sears, clearly puzzled, dismissed any attempt to explore further, by nodding and hurrying through the doorway.

2.

"I nearly lost it, nearly told Sears everything. Everything. I couldn't control it. I'm losing it." Creighton explained to Bonnie in the Ramada Inn's chocolate floored room. "I was so upset, so fraught, so—"

"Forget that. Forget that! Nick's coming here. He wants to see his daughter."

"What? What?"

"I couldn't help it. He's a fucking terror. A fucking terror."

"You couldn't stall him? You couldn't deflect him? What did you tell him?"

"You don't tell Nick. You listen. You don't stall him. You get ready for his coming."

"Here? He's coming here?"

"He's coming unless something better happens."

"Meaning what?"

"Sometimes he stops to buy something, or something more interesting happens."

"You told him where you were?"

"He already knew. He's smart that way."

"Like you."

"Yeah, like me. We're two of a kind. And he's coming here, looking for Sybil. They're two of a kind. Ya see what I mean? He's gonna be pissed when she's not here."

"That's normal."

"He's not normal. Sybil's not normal. Two of a kind. Ya got that? He's a better killer. Much better. She was only learning, beginning to learn . . ."

"And you invited him here. Why?"

"No one invites Nick."

Creighton thought she admires that. She respects his direct action. Maybe she likes his abuse. Could that be? What kind of direction am I capable of? "I nearly lost it with Sears. I wanted to tell him everything. I could barely stop myself—"

"Forget that! Nick's coming here. I couldn't stop him."

Couldn't stop him, couldn't stop myself, Creighton thought, some connection there. Helpless before a rush of self-revilement, a pathetic need to confess to Sears. Ominous emotion. Helpless. He sat down on the chocolate couch and briefly imagined he had squashed Jenna—was she still sleeping there? He swiveled away, quickly put his left leg over the swollen arm of the couch. Let her sleep he imagined, hair quietly spreading out in the tub water. Bubbles stopped. His own left arm bleeding from her clawings. Sears, hear my case: this evil woman led me to atrocity even as I saw it as ultimate liberation. Why couldn't we be groaning toward a new order?

"We need a story to tell Nick. Are you listening?"

And I'm supposed to fashion it? Creighton thought, Why me?

"We'll tell it, or he'll punch it out of us. Ya don't want that. Believe me. You don't want that."

"All right. All right. We've got to tell him a story. Some excuse. Some excuse. Maybe Sybil's on a play date with another girl. Who would that be?"

"Yeah, who the hell might that be?"

"Think of somebody."

"Yeah. Think of somebody. She's on a playdate with somebody's daughter . . . Somebody's dead daughter."

"You're not helping. You're not helping."

"I'm not helping," Bonnie repeated, "God help me, I'm not helping. My sister Aileen came and got Sybil. She's got her. Nick hates her and is scared of her."

"Scared?"

"She put a restraining order on him once, and she's got friends—police friends."

"So, Sybil's with Aileen. Where is Aileen?"

"How the fuck should I know? I haven't seen her in two years."

"So, she came out of nowhere to visit you and took your daughter? To where? Some place nearby?"

"Maybe back on the train to St. Louis? The last I knew she lived there, or near it."

Creighton thought, hear it or near it, hear it or near it, but said, "Okay. Okay maybe he'll buy it."

"He's a dumb shit, but kind of sharp on getting what he wants. Probably money."

"He wants money?"

"He always wants money. His habit. He'd try to sell the T.V. from this room if he got a chance."

"Aileen came and got her and is taking her for the weekend in . . . in where?" Creighton persisted.

"Some place out of state, a good ways away. Maybe North Carolina, some place way west."

"But where?"

"Murphy, North Carolina."

"Why there?"

"I spent a night there once. At the Cricket Motel. Aileen took her for a play date with her child in Murphy."

"She has a child?"

"I don't know. We'll give her one."

"Your sister suddenly has a child?"

"It's more than possible. Let me tell ya.".

"Okay then, Sybil's gone with Aileen to Murphy, North Carolina . . . . And she asked Jenna to come along with her. They played so well together."

"For an extended playdate."

"And in Murphy, Sybil will kill Jenna. Will get her fondest wish and toughest test? Is that it?"

"Nick might like it. He liked to teach Sybil to kill. What's the toughest test?"

"The one we took, and the one we passed, didn't we? With flying, unconscious colors. Didn't we?"

"We had no choice."

"Don't be ridiculous. We chose. They surely didn't, did they? Maybe we should tell Nick that."

"Are you fucking nuts? Give Nick something like that and he'll drain out everything we've got."

"What have we? This shag carpet? These bamboo table lamps? This stupid glass topped coffee table?"

"Jesus! What's wrong with you?"

"There's lots wrong with me. Can't you see that? Or maybe seeing that isn't so important. What's more important is the story we tell to cover what we did. You remember what we did, don't you?"

"You better calm down."

"Maybe we should wake the girls up so they can play with Nick?"

"You're such an asshole."

"No. You go ahead and wake the girls up. If they sleep too much, they'll never get to sleep tonight, and that will surely spoil our plans. So please wake them up."

"You're not funny. Believe me, Nick won't find you funny."

Creighton thought, On the contrary, I'm a laugh riot. On the contrary no one ever thought of me as a comedian. Too focused. Too something else.

"When Nick comes you get the door. You meet him first. That will throw him off. Unbalance him, giving us a chance."

"I don't understand."

"He'll have to behave till he gets set again."

"Behave?"

"He won't take over. It will throw him, for a while anyway."

"Takeover?"

"Can you take a punch?"

"What?"

"You ever been hit? In the face?"

"No. Never. . . . Maybe once in high school. Just out of range. It killed my front tooth. See?" Creighton pointed to a darkened tooth beneath his nose.

"You're such a dipshit," Bonnie said. "Nick'll eat you alive." She seemed amused by the possible scene. "Nick always said, I'd throw in with losers. He always said it." She started a nervous chuckle. "Fucking catastrophe is coming, fucking catastrophe," she said shaking her head.

3.

For another half hour Creighton sat on the couch while Bonnie worked on her appearance in the bathroom. Creighton nudged at his dead tooth and remembered how the punch that killed it was just out of fully- extended arm range. That probably saved him an implant at some point. Was that lucky, he wondered? Luckier than asking Sears for absolution. Yes, luckier than that.

The knocking was appropriately vigorous, resonant. And when Creighton cracked the door, the voice came from higher up than he expected.

"Bonnie here?" Nick asked.

Chapter Four

The crabapple trees of Connecticut came into Solomon Sears' memory whenever the fall weather in D.C. shed its humid miasma and pricked the recesses of his nasal passages. It was like the first nip on a greenish tiny crabapple yanked off the nearest branch. Squirting sourness lifted the lid of thin greyness in celebration of possible liberation. Spiritual flight beyond the tree-etched slate sky. Kite-jerked ascents toward some blueness that had comfort and closeness. Could it be, Sears wondered, that nature would actually rescue us? And from what? The automatic rhetoric of a career already beyond its string? Crab apple twinge as ultimate deliverance? So long as I'm chewing I'm not thinking. And not thinking was revelry. But wasn't nature dying? Nature frying . . . burning off its very life stem, searing the air and water— left unarmed and assaulted in baked vulnerability. Oh hapless nature, fashioning viruses to save itself.

As if to conspire in his revelry his wife Ava had set out her favorite small, brown ceramic bowl filled with crabapples, some with odd, dark protrusions.

"You carry me back to Lime Rock with these gems," Sears shouted beyond the dark mahogany dining table toward the swinging door to the kitchen.

"It means we never have to go back there again," she answered.

"I understand your loathing."

Holding a denim dish towel wrapped like and bandage or maybe a boxing glove around her right hand, Ava pushed the door into the room. "Oh, that town was and is charming . . . . It's the people."

"It's always the people. Racers all." Sears acknowledged.

"Not so much racers but judges, careful measurers of equivalent acquisitions. Your engine versus theirs, or horses, or club memberships. The comparative chit lists of despair."

To lessen the impression "chit lists of despair" had on him Sears asked, "Did you cut your hand?"

"Only my heart every time you mention Lime Rock.'"

"I would not cut your heart for anything, except perhaps it had anti-bodies to tame the virus."

"There are no antibodies for Lime Rock."

"So let's acknowledge that and move on. I didn't get my test today. Did you?"

"I did, and it was wonderful. A simple spit-in-the-cup test and I knew before I drove out of the lot. Negative."

"I had a less thrilling seminar experience, but maybe a scarier one." Sears moved to the credenza at the end of the room and ritually poured himself a sherry from the smudged decanter. "After my best, actually my inspired closing—don't ask what it was, I can't remember. But it was a dazzler, the kind talked about on the way out. After that magnificent effort, there was, inevitably, the after-seminar straggler. The fellow who sidles up to you and brays praise as prelude to some stupid question. And there he was, on cue, so to speak.

Primed and ready, so to speak, and there I was all reception and frenzied anticipation, waiting like a leopard for this antelope to lick me, attempt flight, and stumble into death. But there wasn't the anticipated praise. Indeed, just a straight-out blurting: 'Professor Sears, I want to apologize for my inattention. My two-year-old daughter died yesterday in a grotesque accident. I'm totally unhinged.'"

"Died, did you say, died?"

"That's what he said. Died. My daughter died."

"And he still came to the seminar?"

"He did. And that's what he said."

"And what did you say?"

"I didn't know what to say, so, stupidly, I asked for details."

"Of course, that would be your interest. Not condolence, just interest. Death's gossip."

"I did say I was sorry," Sears insisted. "But, again stupidly, I asked for details, even as I knew that was thoughtless. We're curious creatures, aren't we?"

"Only you, Solly. Only you. So what did he answer?"

"He didn't. After what seemed a pretty long while he just said, 'Sorry, sorry,' slowly."

"And you left it at that? A little girl dead and you left it, floating along on its own weight."

"It was a conversation stopper. It's too early for crabapples. Where did you get them?"

"I didn't get them. Nora gave them to me," Ava answered, apparently allowing the conversation to get off target. And Sears felt relief, but not for long. "Just because some administrator said you would be required to report, that's why you said nothing more. Don't deny it."

"Lately I don't deny anything."

"I know that dodge. What do you know about the accident?"

"Nothing."

"Nothing will come of nothing. Speak again."

"Ah, Madam Lear, you'll get nothing further from me this day."

"At least I'll get the satisfaction of your admitting reporting responsibilities prevented you from inquiring deeper into the so called 'accident.'"

"In truth having to report what I knew about a child's death never entered my mind. I just burrowed into the awkwardness of listening to someone recount the death of his daughter less than three years old."

"You said two years old."

"Details. Worthless details."

"More likely corroborations."

Sears thought but didn't say, Always a lawyer. Always.

And now in full prosecutorial mode he heard her say, "And when the seminar meets, tomorrow doesn't it?"

"Yes."

"And when it meets next you will get the details, clearing you of reporting duties."

"How clearing? Seems like quite the opposite."

"I know what I'm talking about. You need an absolutely clear narrative. Absolutely clear. Do I have to come with you?"

"As much as I might want your company, I don't think that will be necessary."

"Lately I worry that you don't really know what's necessary and what's not."

Sears sat down on his chair at the table. "You're right, of course. Neither of us knows what's necessary in his term 'grotesque accident.' I'll try to find that out. Is that enough so that we can go ahead and plan our marvelous trip to Lime Rock?"

"Very funny."

"I thought we had fun in Lime Rock."

"Only when we joined in invidious comparisons. The place is soul-less."

"Let's go back and talk about Nora's dropping off these hideous crabapples." He poured a second sherry.

2.

Much later when they were in bed Sears had yet another sherry from his oval double walled glass he kept on the nightstand. "You know," he said smiling "sometimes I think we're Stacy Keach and Sarah Miles holding eight ounces each of cream sherry and talking about the uselessness of discussing the world."

"I was wrong to press you on the duty of reporting. I forgot you're not an officer of the court, only a lecturer for half-interested students."

"Is that supposed to make me feel better?"

"Only to bring some proper perspective on what's important."

"And what is important? Beyond a trip to Lime Rock?"

"It might be important to find out what happened to that two-year-old girl. Maybe important enough to save her."

"I'd like to save her. Saving her feels good."

"Saving her might redeem our bored life, eating crab apples—"

"More likely not eating them. Spitting them out."

"Yes, spitting them out. Like the shards of our life."

"I like your moroseness. It's somehow gratifying." He set the glass back down on the nightstand, momentarily wondering if it would leave a ring stain on the mirror finish of the mahogany. Then he turned to her, pinned her with his left arm across her right arm and shoulder and kissed her, pressing hard. His tongue finding hers. He was surprised she seemed suddenly receptive, so he followed up, whispering: "Fuck Lime Rock." His left arm unpinned and now exploring between her legs.

She guided his hand and whispered back, "Yes Lime Rock needs it."

"Let's save Lime Rock," he answered.

Later, he said. "Listen, I've been thinking how we might get shut of the mask and test routine."

"Go back to sleep."

"No. Listen to this. We've not signaled respect for Covid. We need to do that, and I've found the best possible way. Ava, I know the way. Listen to this.

"Turn over. Ease back into sleep. Let it go."

"No, you've got to hear this, try this. It's our path out of fear."

"There's no fear."

"Fear unrecognized counts even more. Listen to this plan. Listen to my words."

"Jesus, go back to sleep. If you wake me up, you'll regret it. Deeply."

"Don't you think I know that? Of course I know that. But let me give you the path. The sunlit path out of the forest."

"Jesus, how poetic."

"It is poetic. Listen to this. We've been told wear masks even when making love, having sex. We need to respect that. Deeply respect that. I want you to put a mask over your luscious mound of love. Tape its flexible straps to your luscious stomach and then on the back taped to your creamy bottom. A mask of Venus over the entrance of joy, the gate of delirium."

"Jesus . . ."

"Maybe with just the beginning of a tiny slit in the center of the mask, the faint aluminum bar pinched softly over the crest of mound, and then I ease through the mask, unable to tear it, sliding through its tissue filter and begin a soft rhythm that sets the mask sighing. Respectful sighing. Together we pay the mask ultimate respect in the crescendo of our mating so that no droplets get exchanged. They cannot leak out beyond the mask. Droplets depend entirely on the shaft of delivery. The mask holds tight, no other entry. Purity maintained even as heightened frenzy prevails. "

"Frenzy?"

"Imagine it."

"You missed Junior High school, didn't you?"

"This is reverence for science. This is serious love, masked and appropriate."

"And what tape are you thinking of for attachment to my luscious stomach and creamy backside?"

Sears thought a minute and finally settled on something that made him smile broadly, "Duct tape?"

"Try Frog tape, or artist's masking tape."

"Then you go for it? You agree to pay homage to science in the most serious way. We slay the mask in aspiration of a new world of populous—mask-made children."

"At least one of whom has been cruelly butchered. I can hear her choking and sobbing. I recommend double-thick Frog tape . . . over your mouth, not mine." She turned over.

Imagined mask-tearing fornication for Sears was almost as good as achieving his longing. He surprised himself by closing his eyes over sparkling microns descending across his hardening eyeballs and nodded off almost immediately.

He might have hoped for dreams of large ballerinas in too tight tutus but all that occurred was the soft winding sound of the blue toned electronic clock in the thick, furry darkness into which he sunk sweetly. Paddling through gingerspiced oil. Was this the death he knew Covid secreted about his unrecognized premises? Door handles he couldn't quite reach? Relatives waving him, or some other spectral souls just behind him, calling him on? Summoning Solomon to the very lintel of something or other. "Here, Solly, I will set you free. No need to fret about someone else's butchery. Here care slides into pure slalom relief. Look, watch the chains dissolve the leather straps shrivel in embarrassment at ever holding anything. Look the little girls frolic on the longest imaginable slide. Join them. Push your nose or dick through the crinkly mask."

3.

In the morning over hot oatmeal slathered with maple sugar, Ava returned to the issue: "You have a human obligation— new concept for you—yes, a human obligation to explore what was really going on with that fellow."

"And you're the card-carrying human?"

"Recognition's half the battle."

"Touché. I'll talk to him."

"Probably he won't want to talk. You lost your chance. There was just a moment when he needed to share, and you shut him down. Very predictable. Now it's too late."

"So, I should give it up?

"Listen to yourself. Avoidance. Denial. Giving up. You're normal mode. Do what you want, since you will anyway."

"As a mentor you're something of a flop."

"You need, and maybe I need, to inquire after it. Maybe, just maybe, there's a little girl's life on the line."

"How could you possibly imagine she's alive?"

"You know why."

He exhaled and took a long sip of his morning tea, Mincing Lane. He did know why. "Should we allow our disappointments to run all our perceptions?"

"I'm simply saying nobody just announces death the way he did. Not of his own child."

"Is there an etiquette of death announcing?"

"It struck me as you retold it, he was asking for help and you, characteristically, missed the message. You're a lousy listener. A much better pontificator."

"It comes with the job."

"With you it was natural. But I'm serious. You need to follow up. You know all too well what this state does to prove any child's death was accidental. Any miscarriage was not intentional. Do I have to remind you?"

"Of course not. Of course not."

"So do your duty. Find out what happened. Use our experience as a weapon to force him to open up."

Sears waited a moment then said, "Ah, some purpose in our sadness. Some useful benefit. I don't believe it. Neither do you. We're stuck, aren't we? Deservedly stuck." He fingered the crab apples. The bowl had been moved from the entry to the chipped porcelain topped kitchen table. His fourth finger rested on the largest brown protrusion. He tapped it lightly and waited for her rejoinder.

Chapter Five

Creighton had thought, if it's Nick, the knock is suspiciously faint, suspiciously tentative. He's supposed to be a strong boy, colossal aggressor, so why the shy knock? Perhaps it's only the staff wanting to vacuum the room?

"Don't answer it," Bonnie had said.

"What if it's just the maid?"

"Believe me, it's not the maid."

But Creighton had already reached the door and partially opened it.

The voice was suspiciously soft, "Bonnie here?" Nick said with a certain disarming tentativeness.

Creighton had to look up to the black shaggy beard almost above the door lintel. He thought about lying, thought about feigning irritated anger at the violation of his private, single room. Could he carry it off? Maybe, but he knew the convincing would collapse under Nick's imagined interrogation. So Creighton capitulated with, "Yes, of course, we've been waiting for you."

Creighton imagined Nick actually ducked coming through the door. Once inside it seemed he filled the room. A Greek Orthodox prophet, Creighton thought, with an enviable Hebrew super beard. Hands larger than boxing gloves and the odor of a stale sauna in some Russian train stop beyond the Urals, or, more likely, in the highest hillside of Chechnya, or so Creighton fantasized. He had never been to either place.

"Where's my Sybil?" Nick said slowly, looking around."

"She's not here," Bonnie answered in a strange sing-song voice.

"I can see that. Where is she?"

Creighton suddenly thought, we're still setting that up yet. All that planning and we're still learning our lines.

"Pre-school. She gets out after nap, around 2:30." Bonnie said in the same sing-song voice, amazing Creighton. Murphy, North Carolina tossed into oblivion?

"Why the fuck didn't you tell me that?" Nick said.

"It came up after we talked," with, again, quick, responsive harshness.

"Don't play fucking games with me, Bonnie."

"No games. You can pick her up 2:30. I signed you in as her father. You have permission to get her."

"Where's the school?"

"1410 Rhode Island, on the other side of D.C. Takes about twenty minutes to walk there, or you can taxi it in six or seven minutes. Do you take taxis?"

"Fuck you. And who's this rube?"

"Creighton. Sybil's with my daughter, Jenna . . . at the school. I'll meet you there." Creighton smiled and thought about nodding, as if he'd just shared a gambling tip, which he had.

For a long difficult moment Nick studied both of them, then said to Creighton, "You can fuck her if you like. She's easy—"

"Goodbye, Nick." Bonnie said, opening the door.

There was another long, difficult moment. Creighton instinctively moved his left foot back as if to absorb a punch. He relived the high school blow, just out of range enough to save his front tooth's root but not its nerve.

Nick said from the hallway just loud enough that rooms down to the elevators could have heard, "You can still fuck her, if you want."

Creighton watched from the door jamb and when Nick got into the sticky bronze elevator he turned back to Bonnie and asked. "The pre-school actually exists?"

"Yes!"

"At the address you gave him?"

"Of course! I tried to enroll her when we first got here. But, get this, they wanted about fifteen thousand dollars just to sign her up. I told 'em I'd have to talk to my financial people."

"And you did, and they threw up."

'Yes! That's good!" Bonnie laughed. "But now we've got to leave D.C. We've got to go away. When Nick gets to the school, we've got to be gone. Absolutely gone! You following?"

Creighton was thinking,—No, you've got to be gone. I can stay, perhaps with a little protection, but I can stay. I've earned staying. Suddenly and for the first time he felt detached from what had happened. We are not the same. I had obligations, professional duties, and a seminar to participate in. People were interested in my perceptions. People understood I had grasped issues they were confused about. I could illuminate policy differences, suggest new compromises, new ways forward. How absurd the phrase sounded. He comically imagined Nick listening to such "new ways forward". Would Nick take notes? Creighton began shuttered interior laughter.

"It's not funny, nothing funny," Bonnie said. "You don't understand the threat Nick is. The length he'll go to get his little girl back. Not that he gives a shit about her. It's what he thinks about himself that will kill us. And believe me he'll kill us, when he finds out, he'll kill us."

"More likely, he'll kill you," Creighton said with a strange, measured coolness. He smiled and stifled further muffled laughter. A threatening situation always elicited from Creighton deep seeded chuckling—a way to distance from any contemplated negative outcome. The more precarious the situation the stronger the laughter, always beginning interiorly, but eventually uncontrollably in the triumph of mirth over terror. Mirth over terror. Was that the new touchstone of a happy life—a life in which one could accept a certain personality separation? Was separation the right word? Maybe two sides of the same donut? An eminently squeezable donut. His teeth in the Krispy Kreme forced out chocolate deliciousness embarrassing him before the line awaiting their delights. He bit before he paid, Creighton thought, and for that I will suffer greatly. Greatly. Ah, woe is laughing me.

2.

Now confidant that Nick was headed toward the school, Creighton sat on the couch, his knees edging the shell studded coffee table's glass top further into the combo living/sleeping room.

"What do you figure we have? Maybe four hours in which to disappear forever?'

"Our last golden hours before butchery," Bonnie said, half laughing.

"And still with no place to go," Creighton added. "Maybe we should go west into empty lands and start a new family there in the wind-swept plains, or maybe at the foothills of the Rockies. The Great Rocky Mountains . . . Surely there's someplace for us to hide."

"Hide till when?" Bonnie asked.

"How'd he find you here?"

"Talking to people. He's clever that way, relentless. Just kept asking as if he had genuine interest and could convince anyone how much he missed his daughter."

But Creighton no longer seemed interested in the conversation. Instead, he stood up and walked to the tiny kitchenette area and propped himself with stiff arms on the faded blue-green linoleum. "Jesus this is so fifties," he said scratching at the surface. "What if Nick isn't real, just God's way of wondering why we drowned our kids."

"Horse shit," Bonnie said. "Pure horseshit. Nick's plenty real, especially when he kicks your head off, which he will."

"Maybe we deserve that," Creighton said. "Isn't it the greatest sin? Isn't it?"

"I can think some greater . . . like . . . like Hiroshima, or this shitty pandemic." Bonnie answered.

"Those are stupid social sins, societal miss steps, I'm talking about us. You and me, and . . . and Sybil and Jenna. Good God, Bonnie, Sybil and Jena, in a black garbage bag at the bottom of the Atlantic someplace in the Bermuda Triangle. Can't you see it? Writhing to get us to free them. Can't you hear them at night moaning and crying and clutching at salted plastic strangling them. We never even checked to see if they were dead, did we? We never even knew for sure, did we . . . Did we?"

"Of course you feel regret. I do too. That's natural, but what's done is done. And maybe we didn't really do it ourselves. The drugs helped, didn't they? And besides we can't undo it, so we have to find a way to go on living. No brooding about something we didn't entirely understand, even as we did it. Didn't we know we'd live through it? How could we do it, if we didn't know we'd be okay with it. And we are okay with it. We're here now, we're okay with it, so get used to being okay with it. Blame it on the drugs, if that helps, but get beyond it. And focus on the immediate threat. Nick's going to kill us when he gets to the school and they tell him she never enrolled. Then he's gonna come looking for us and when he finds us . . . . It won't be pretty. It won't be easy. He'll make us envy Sybil and Jenna. That's what's ahead. Focus on that. Get beyond that. We couldn't have saved them just ourselves from Nick. We saved them somehow didn't we? Didn't we?"

"That's absurd."

"No! We're absurd. You're absurd mired in moaning over what we actually did. Not caring a shit about what's coming. Right until it gets here and wipes us out. So we gotta get packed and get away from here. We've got to find secret shelter.

"Secret shelter," Creighton repeated the phrase slowly, as if directly imagining it. "Secret shelter, if we could actually find it. Wouldn't that be extraordinary. Out of the ordinary. Way out of the ordinary. That's what's important isn't it?"

"Just shut up and get packed. I'm already packed. We gotta get out of here. Now!"

"Jenna just wants to be safe. Safe and sound and not afraid. She was always so afraid."

"Look, stop fixing on it. Stop it now. Now! We gotta clear this place and no trace left behind. Do you understand? Not a trace. Nick will find us. And when he does there won't be any secret shelter. None whatsoever. None. We gotta leave now."

"Sometimes I could give her that shelter. Some times."

"We can eat in the car. I know a Chinese takeout place. We gotta go." She pushed him toward his open baggage on the rack at the end of the couch. "I'll get your stuff from the bathroom. Focus on getting out."

"We'll pick up Jenna after lunch," Creighton said slowly, stuffing a shirt into his bag. "She'll have eaten. She and Sybil won't need lunch."

Bonnie despaired of offering him verbal directions. She helped him close his bag, helped him slip it off the baggage holder, pulled up the metal handle enabling him to wheel the bag toward the door. She muscled her duffle bag's strap over her left shoulder and looked, suddenly longingly at the disheveled bed and the abandoned small cups near the coffee maker.

3.

Thirty-five minutes later they shared egg rolls and a double order of General Tso's Chicken off a plastic tray in their rented "Mazda 5, parked beside an enormous blue dumpster behind the takeout restaurant. Bonnie was fascinated that Creighton seemed oblivious to the fiery pale-yellow mustard he kept smearing on the bitten end of his egg roll. Between bites he recreated what he claimed was a constant dream/vision.

"Jenna in black garbage bag shards walks toward me out of a brackish dark green sea, holding her arms out to me and shouting, "Daddy, lift me out of the water. Stop pushing me down. You're my father, my whole guarantor of life, Lift me up, please, Daddy, please. And as she is begging me, I can see that she is growing taller and fuller and eventually menacing, with enormous tentacle-like arms, dripping thick brown oil from their edges. You couldn't save me, could you? Daddy you couldn't save me, could you? So now I must save you. Come here, my father, my alleged savior, let me embrace you and steal you out of your garden of distraction, out of your prison of distraction."

"What the fuck are you talking about?" Bonnie said.

"Our prison of distraction. Wasn't that why we did it. Of course it was. We were lost in our distractions, believing every moment could be redeemed in dismissal with some perfect or imagined perfect, distraction. And we knew before we knew that the only way out of our prison of distraction was to commit some unfathomable atrocity—we could kill our way to deliverance couldn't we? Wasn't that so, Bonnie? We could escape the mirror world of distraction by taking the sharpest, most savage course, toward some unthinkable act of butchery beyond the very categories we lived in. Isn't that so?"

"And what do ya now have in mind?" Bonnie asked. With a white plastic spoon she eased a particularly chewy piece of chicken, thickened with brown batter, into her mouth. "Does Jenna with tenacles still use a spoon?"

Creighton answered only by repeating, "Daddy why are you pushing me down? You know I have to breathe. Why are you taking that from me now? Why? Isn't it possible, Bonnie, that we imagined we were saving them from our universe of meaningless distractions? Isn't that possible?"

"Nah, not possible," Bonnie answered flatly. "Finish your egg roll."

He did so, bolstered by her sternness, alert to a sense of sullenness that seemed relief to him. He believed he could be distracted or sullen, but not both at once and that seemed freeing. A warmth toward Bonnie welled up in him, and he consciously fought down a smile toward her. When the last smidgeon of mustard had been swallowed so that the stinging in his throat and nose seemed in need of another dose to keep him occupied, he suddenly realized there was at least a temporary solution to their desperation.

"I know where we can spend the night and Nick can't find us," he said to Bonnie with a conviction that surprised her.

Part II

Deterrence and Force
Preponderance

Chapter Six

Soft breezes, hot wet nights, and constant screaming. Seaman Apprentice Carleton in charge. Nick listening for clues, or just figuring it out. What did it mean—a quarter flipped on the cot's blanket? Bouncing. Something about the quarter bouncing. No second bouncing. One bounce. "And then no more!" No more! Or was that in the morning? At night one bounce and then no more! One bounce as you got into the cot. One bounce. Only one bounce. In the morning only one bounce of the quarter. At night one bounce only from your own body on the mattress. One only.

And in the morning more than one bounce meant duck walks around the barracks. Duck walks until you threw up. No second bounce. Second bounce meant duck walks till you threw up. One bounce. One bounce. One quarter and one bounce. No second bounce.

Seaman Apprentice Carleton in command, so young and smiling. Smiling as he made 100 men duck walk till they threw up. Seaman Apprentice Carleton so much younger than his duck walkers. And yet with all command powers. Duck walk till you puke. Or high port your rifle until your shoulders turned to fiery jello. Or do pushups until you passed out and rolled over on your back while Carleton put his right foot on your chest, and slowly walked across you. And smiling, laughing at your grimace. Beardless, savage Carleton, amazed at what he could command. Get down. Get up. Down for pushups. Duck walk. Puke. Playing with his 100 puppets. Smug in his authority, drunk on his omnipotence.

On the second night long after lights out Nick was alone in the head sitting in a stall and swallowing the last vomit down, when he heard soft voices whispering over faucet water running. Then quiet footsteps toward the exit, then stopping and a glass wall case opening—access to the fire-hose with its heavy brass nozzle. Then snickers as the nozzle was being unscrewed. Nick waited another twenty seconds to make sure the head was empty, and eased open the stall door. He stepped out. Too late to realize they had not left. Four of them, the Coast Guard's lone black recruits in the 100-man company initial bootcamp contingent, Fox Trot 87. The tallest one looked directly at Nick and said, "You're with us now. You're in. Get over here."

"In for what?" Nick asked, conscious that he was larger, perhaps stronger than any of them. He moved toward the group and thought about getting possession of the brass nozzle, the only weapon at hand.

"For C-boy's blanket party." One of them said. "We're gonna take him out."

"No more duck walks," another said. "You're in. No way out. You're in. Raj says you're in. You're in." He tossed the dark khaki blanket to Nick.

It felt warm and wiry, suitably harsh. Nick figured C-boy was Carleton. He was less sure what a "blanket party" entailed. Lots of pain and doubtless some use of the nozzle. For a moment Nick imagined he might overpower the tall one, intimidate the others into fleeing. But that would save C-boy and duck walks. C-boy gets broken or duck walks continued. Easy choice. Nick unfolded the blanket and hung it on his left arm, and nodded. Raj smiled. Nick imagined he had lent muscle to the mission and more confidence. They exited the head turned left down the corridor for petty officers' rooms. C-boy alone spent the night in the Foxtrot barracks. His door was four inches ajar and was soundlessly pushed further open. The blanket was lifted off of Nick's arm. Raj moved to the far side of Carleton's cot. Two others took noiseless positions at the foot of the cot and held their hands about three inches above Carleton's ankles. Raj motioned to open the blanket slowly, and pass edges of it above Carleton so that eventually it seemed only a thick canopy suspended above a sleeping child who, on his side seemed almost girl-ish in his soft vulnerability. Raj nodded once, twice, and on the third head jerk dropped his edge and clamped the top of the falling blanket over Carleton's mouth and head. The bottom edge of the blanket clamped onto to his ankles and immediately the giant nozzle flailed down on the mid-point of the blanket. cracking Carleton's rib cage, then flailed again rupturing his left thigh and snapping his kneecap that had involuntarily turned upward in response to the chest pain. One more swooping crack mangled the other kneecap. Carleton's moaning was only a whimpered agony through the clamping gag of the blanket, Raj's hands, elbows arms and shoulder keeping the khaki shroud in place. Carleton remained immobilized; a weird wheezing moan sounded from C-boy's mouth through the blanket. Raj nodded to-ward the shins and twice more the nozzle slammed down, crushing bones with crinkling snapping sound. Nick stood dumbfounded at the quickness of the attack. Carleton appar-ently had passed out or perhaps he was terrified more noise would elicit another strike. Raj nodded and the team darted noiselessly out the room, returned to the head, and watched as Nick screwed the nozzle back onto the folded hose. Raj eased the glass door shut and motioned everyone back to the barracks.

A few minutes later Carleton's sobbing screams awakened the entire squad bay. But everyone lay unspeaking in darkness until an ambulance arrived and three EMTs rolled a gurney into Carleton's room. And unfamiliar voice bellowed at the squad bay's opening, "Reveille is 5:15. Goodnight Ladies."

By morning chow Nick understood that blanket parties were routine, and Carleton had crossed some commonly accepted abuse line and therefore his suffering was unremarkable. What was remarkable was how quickly it had come and with such professional silence—a threat to whomever would take command of Foxtrot 87. C-boy had command of Fox Trot 87 in its initial forming. The designated C.O. would have to be careful.

But Bosunmate Moulton wasn't. The word in the squad bay was that Nick, since he was the largest and evidently the strongest must have been at least a key part of Carleton's butchery.

Moulton himself asserted as much to Nick in a private meeting outside the barracks. Nick didn't deny it, impressed that no justice, no investigation, no response, had been undertaken. Evidently brute force wrote the rules.

Moulton explained, "You're my enforcer. Got that? I tell you to tune somebody up and you do it. In return nobody bothers you and you get your own room. And if you do it well, I get you liberty before the others. It's not a bargain. You do it, or I make it hell for you here. Got that? A living hell."

"A living hell," Nick repeated.

"American hell is better than a Samoan hell," Nick's father had said. "Leave now and join." It was an unacknowledged statement between father and son, that the American armed forces offered a path out of a broken family in an impoverished village, a life imagined without prospects for a future festooned with Hollywood images of surfeit and joy. Hie thee, then, son, to Elysium. To Fort something in America's blessed state of New Jersey. Only it wasn't a fort, but only a Coast Guard barracks with 100 tenants living out of seabags strapped to a central pipe. 100 bags. 100 men, and two in separate rooms—Moulton and Nick Tamaroa apparently in command. Strapping Nick Tamaroa, 6'5 inches. Moulton much shorter and much louder. Moulton radiated energy, performed a perfect frenzy of command. He could prance backward, high porting his rifle and exhorting his hapless troops to greater effort. Nick emanated sloth, relaxation and occasional ferocity camouflaged by evident docility. Nick didn't march, didn't fall-in, didn't muster. He was a human ICBM resting in his silo of threat on Moulton's behalf. And gradually Nick understood the favorite exercise among the troops was the guessing game of who among them would get to take on Nick and thus destroy Moulton's authority. In that game Nick understood he needed to mollify his black conspirators—keep them from imagining a blanket party for Nick. He fed them sticks of gum that Moulton had given him as incentive toward loyalty. Much more effectively Nick offered them the prospect, if not the reality, of early liberty.

Within the barracks Nick recognized he'd reached celebrated status. A new fear underscored as he got his own room and could stand outside formation awaiting Moulton's directives to discipline the 100 disciples. At night he could stroll out of the barracks, an almost unimaginable freedom for the rest of Foxtrot 87. Often after lights out he exited the barracks and headed through the marching practice fields to the ocean; the relentless lapping sound seemed a calming force. He would scuff along the water's edge. Cape May's distant night lights a soft glowing globe to his right. He stared at the sullen water and summoned up memories of the fierce blue-green of Vatic bay and the camaraderie of passing around a thick bottle of Shochu and the now silly summonings of American fulfillment. His father got him passage to the alleged finest, and only, place of American recruitment training, the American Coast Guard Base at Cape May, New Jersey. "The best journey is never direct," his father said before Nick left.

Nick listened to the gentle swill of the ocean and kept watch mentally for the most likely barracks challenger. He believed it would be the one nearly as tall as Nick and muscular enough from daily workouts. The one named Shelton who seemed as hostile as Moulton and as threatening. It seemed eddies of adulation flowed around Shelton in the barracks, and it would only be a matter of time before he would accept resentment's tide forward to challenge Nick's designated authority.

Moulton mentioned the challenge would be coming and counseled Nick never to turn his back. Nick fixed on the strange smile Moulton wore explaining what would happen, how it would unfold. "You'll handle it. Just end it quickly, decisively. No second round. No corner retreat. End it so no one would doubt what happened, no one would doubt how it had happened. That's leadership. That's sweet triumph. He thinks he's a boxer. So take him down with a wrestling move. Just take him down and out. Don't feel him out. Just flatten him. They'll remember."

Five evenings later, just after the slow recitation of the Coast Guardsmen's Prayer, Shelton stepped to the center space between the two lines of troops in their underwear. "You're the tough guy," Shelton shouted toward Nick. "You're supposed to enforce the rules, but I say Fuck That! We don't need you pretending to do Boat's work. Fuck That! I say Fuck this enforcer!"

Nick came into the center space about twenty feet away from Shelton. He advanced toward him, feeling his heart pumping faster, his core tightening. He was slightly taller than Shelton. That felt like an advantage. Nick weighed standing up, inviting a boxing stance, but kept advancing slowly. The line of troops seemed frozen just searching the still air for some signal of combat.

"How tough are you?" Shelton taunted, shifting his right foot back a bit. "So fucking tough. Come on."

The gap between them closed and it seemed there would be a conversation or mutual, expected swearing, but Nick watched Shelton' fist closing, and, with amazing suddenness, squatted and dove forward, a spearing thrust so that his shoulders rammed into Shelton's thighs as Nick shot his hands behind Shelton's knees and pulled forward and upwards, swiveling him to the left and into the suspended seabags which magically parted. Rising further and shoving ferociously Nick sent Shelton's lifted body into the opening, slamming the back of Shelton's head against the ringing pipe, soon dappled with Shelton's blood and inert form which Nick let topple to the deck, between leaping troops getting out of the way. Empty frightened space embraced Shelton's broken moaning beneath the returning bags like a curtain closing over a dispatched hero. Nick turned and looked down the frozen line, as if to invite the next challenge.

Moulton had come out of his room. Light flooded the squad bay. "Get towels and ambulance," he shouted. "Now for Chrissakes now! Now!"

After lights out, Moulton came into Nick's room and stood in front of Nick sitting on the cot, "Pretty fucking impressive," Moulton said, softly, smiling. "You made your point nicely. Followed the script, just like I told you. Liberty coming up. Maybe even this weekend."

Nick registered Moulton was afraid, and that made Nick feel better about the effort. Better but not heartened. Within a week Nick heard mutterings, ruminations over who should be the next challenger. The chatter seemed to center on a short Southerner named Gabbon—that might have been a first or a last name. Short and muscularly husky and quick, dartingly quick, Gabbon had legendary staying power, tireless, relentless, or so it passed along sideways among the marching troops. Nick watched and listened from a distance and wedged his boondockers in the bottom hinge of his door at night for protection. He upped the gum delivery to his black fellow combatants.

On the second following weekend Moulton granted liberty to Nick and even drove him from bootcamp to the bar strip of Wildwood opposite a run down USO facility in a brown clapboard building. He handed Nick seven fifty-dollar bills and told him where to buy some civilian pants a shirt and shoes and most importantly a baseball cap to hide his bootcamp brush cut. "Have some fun. Get back by oh eight hundred Monday. And get ready for the next challenge."

"You mean Gabbon?"

"Probably, but sometimes new guys suddenly pop up. Yeah, probably Gabbon. So have some fun. You've earned it."

"It's a lot of money," Nick said, fingering the bills.

"Not so much. I've got a sideline I'll cut you in on in a bit, if you keep delivering. Now get going. Liberty has a way of rushing by. And don't be surprised if you're really tired by 10 o'clock. That's what barracks life does to you. Fight it.

Fight it like Gabbon does. He has staying power. It won't be a one-shot takedown."

It was a phrase Nick muttered as he changed clothes in the Goodwill Store. "No one- shot takedown."

He got directions to the bus station and found a Greyhound leaving for New York almost immediately. "No one-shot takedown," he said softly in the narrow, stained seat in the far back left side of the bus . . . Surely Moulton was testing him with so much money. Would he flee, having been given such an easy exit? Or would he come back for even more money in Moulton's alleged sideline? Of course, I'll come back, Nick thought—just after sampling the city that never sleeps. No one-shot takedown. After triumphs in New York, Gabbon would be an easy, off-hand demolition.

2.

The bus's sudden bucking woke Nick from his sweet sleep. The rough jostling as the bus's engine coughed toward collapse ended Nick's drifting, relaxed imagination that he wouldn't return to bootcamp. Facing Gabbon seemed momentarily unreal, and Nick sensed his body untoughening at the prospect of never going back. It seemed as the bus lumbered off the turnpike and limped into Union City's bus station that Moulton had deliberately invited Nick to flee, to exit the soldier enterprise. Why drop so much money on Nick? Was not the kindly father telling his boy to explore the world? And now the broken bus provided the full opportunity, as did the pale green 3 by 5 index card stapled to the cork wall board outside the Union City bus station: "Need a room for the night, please call Bee" with phone number and address listed.

In imagined hope Nick thought Bee ought to be a thirty-three-year-old lithe woman fixed on having her first child with whomever called. But she turned out to be a short black man uninterested in having children.

"You looking to spend the night?"

"Yes!" Nick answered with he realized too much enthusiasm. "Are you Bee?"

"Could be. Why you asking?"

"I thought Bee would be a woman, that's all."

"Twenty-five for the night. You leave before eleven a.m. I'll give you a towel after you pay."

"Do I get a look at the room?"

"No. It's upstairs right opposite the first landing. But you pay first."

As Nick paid, a woman of immense size and wearing an orange flowing light-weight robe came up behind the black man and acknowledged him with a soft enunciation, "Now Buddy," don't overcharge this young man. He has a gentle face and kindly demeanor, don't you think, Buddy?"

"Yes," Buddy said. "I charged the standard rate after 5:30."

"Well, Buddy, he surely looks to me like a 4:00 p.m. person, so give him back his five dollars. We see all too many of the other kind, so give him back his five dollars."

"Yes, Bee." He gave Nick five ones, counting them out slowly for emphasis.

"Now, you come into my parlor," Bee said to Nick, "and sit a spell, while I play." Together they went in the pale green parlor with its distant Baldwin upright piano. Bee pulled off her floppy yellow rubber gloves. "I was either about to do a bunch of laundry, or maybe tidy up the garden—sometimes I lose track of the plan, especially if I have a new guest on the premises." She chuckled and sat down at the piano. "I assume most people like soft piano music, especially as the twilight comes up. Isn't that right, Buddy?" But Buddy had gone elsewhere. "No matter. What is your name, young man?"

"Nick Tamaroa."

"I love exotic names, Nick Tamaroa. I believe you're Polynesian, is that so?"

"Samoan."

"Same diff. I'm good with names. You know why? Because for 34 years I taught Junior High School in Newark. Lots of names across those years and how I struggled to recognize and pronounce them correctly. Correctly, but sweetly. I'll play some Chopin, but you go along to your room, Nick Tamaroa. Buddy will take care of your every need."

"Do you know when the earliest bus leaves for New York City?"

"You don't have to say New York City, New York will suffice. And of course, I really mean suffice. When I retired I took my nephew and his wife (a really strange ugly woman) to the city to see Johnny Mathis. Wonderful concert in a nightclub. My 34 years in Newark's finest middle schools came to an end." She stopped playing, apparently to allow Nick to concentrate on her narrative. "Yes, 34 years of listening to their silent abuse, their utter rejection of all my, indeed our, values. Don't you agree? 'I don't have to do your fucking math.' 'Your math sucks!' and I listened to it and moved through it, always seeking out that little hidden lamp I could, if I were really lucky, might light someday. 'I don't have to listen to your shit.' Not yours of course. Just what I listened to everyday for 34 years."

"That was tough." Nick said, thinking she must at least three hundred and fifty pounds.

"Oh, tough enough. But some days, some very empty days I wish I could hear their foul language. Isn't that odd?

Abuse when you miss it becomes something else, doesn't it?" She watched Nick carefully, and apparently satisfied that her bluntness had untouched him, she resumed playing Chopin. "You run along to your room. You can take a bath—there's no shower—in the little bathroom to the right of the next landing. Buddy should have given you a towel. Did he?"

"Yes, yes . . ."

"You can call me Bee. Sometimes Auntie Bee. My students sometimes did that, if I liked them. And I didn't much. Not much at all."

He decided against a bath and collapsed directly unto the old quilt covering his rather high single bed. He kicked off his shoes and fell asleep.

Around 3:30 a.m. he heard her calling out for Buddy. What began as suitably demanding soon burrowed into frenzied desperation, then choking guttural sounds pierced occasionally by a suddenly clear "Buddy!!" summoning him and everything else to her bedside. "Buddy! Now. Come now! Buddy!"

Nick slipped off his bed and conscious that his socks might slide on the polished floor went up five more steps to the entrance of her bedroom.

"You're not Buddy."

"Yes."

"Well, get him. I'm not going unless he comes too. They'll not take me without Buddy." She turned away and vomited over the far side of bed.

Nick added his screaming voice to the summons of Buddy. And Nick heard scrambling footsteps on the stairs.

Buddy pushed past and half climbed on the bed yanking Bee away from her heaving. "It'll be okay, Bee. Not to worry. It'll be okay. Always is." He pulled her toward the center of the bed.

"Don't lie to me, stinker," Bee answered. "Just call them. Tell them I'll go this time. I know what's happening. Call them." She twisted away from his arms and settled back into the bed. Suddenly she arched back up and scrunching her face let loose with an agonized howl starting from low moan through guttural grinding hacking coughs, spiraling toward a dark whine and then a full scream.

"Jesus!" Buddy shouted and gathered as much of her right shoulder and side as he could manage to envelop and pull into a sitting position. "Jesus!" he shouted again as Nick clearly scented excrement flooding out from the tangled covers of the bed. "Bee? Bee?" Buddy inquired of the slumping figure he half held. But her head flopped so loosely as if disconnected from her body, and the fume of loose shit filled the room. Nick turned away gagging.

Buddy dumped her and scrambled off the bed. "Follow me. Get your stuff. Get your stuff together and meet me in the kitchen."

"You're getting an ambulance?" Nick asked.

"Right," Buddy answered, laughing.

They met in the kitchen and Buddy pointed to the door to the garage. "Put your stuff in the back seat. I'll get the garage open."

There was a rust-colored Chevrolet Malibu Maxx aimed at the door Buddy lifted upwards. When they turned left on to Union's main street, Nick asked "We're getting help?"

"No," Buddy answered, "We're taking this shit bucket to Miami."

Chapter Seven

It was just before midnight when Nick and Buddy reached Denny's Restaurant on NW. 41st St., outside of Miami. Nick had slept most of the previous hours since Buddy seemed energized almost to frenzy by driving. He had no intention of yielding the wheel.

Buddy ordered the fullest breakfast—sausage patties, pancakes, home fries, rye toast, and three refill coffees. Nick had only pancakes and when they were finished Buddy announced they'd sleep in the car till 9 a.m. "They know me here. No problem. Gotta park a long way from the entrance. That's the deal. I've worked it out before."

Nick wondered what else had been worked out before. He watched Buddy ease his seat way back and confident that Buddy was asleep he opened his door and stood outside watching the black sky above Denny's gradually sharpen to pricks of distant lights and overhead sparkling stars. The soft, mucid air was slightly chilly. He smelled the same N.J. ocean in Florida so much warmer and motion-filled than the Vatic Bay he remembered. He pictured his drinking buddies in a ring watching the sullen Pacific night.

And remembering his ring of friends tripped off images of the barracks in Cape May and he wondered if Gabbon might emerge from the group or ring. Surely Gabbon had been designated enforcer for Moulton and Nick wondered if there had been other challengers. It would have to have been someone Moulton was scared of. Nick sorted through applicants. None as big as Nick, none as strong, so he could have gone back, re-assumed his role. Would Buddy drive him back? He'd ask him when he woke up.

Suddenly a pickup truck pulled into Denny's and three young workers stumbled out toward the entrance. They seemed drunk, and Nick watched carefully. None as compact as Gabbon. At the door the last one turned toward Nick and shouted, "No sleeping in the lot!" then laughed and went in.

"I'm not sleeping, asshole," Nick said to the darkness. He got back into the car, eased his seat as far down as it could go and like Buddy drifted into soft snoring.

"No sleeping in the lot!" came the shout again. Was it a memory? A vague hostility from a long line at morning chow? Was it Moulton himself, about to bounce a quarter off Nick's forehead? No, indeed. From someone pawing at Nick's closed window. "No sleeping in the lot!"

Nick rammed his door open shoving the shouter back awkwardly, who stumbled to keep erect and Nick stood outside the car. He watched as the other two seemed impressed by his size. There was a pause in which everything seemed frozen.

Finally, the newly balanced fellow apparently conveyed a sudden consensus among the three, "Sorry," he said quietly.

"Sorry?" Nick asked in equal quietness, gathering his core for a lunge. He figured he could put two of them down in such a charge, leaving the smallest for either running away or quick demolition.

It seemed they recognized a train coming and instinctively raised their hands. "He's just shit faced. Meant nothing. No problems here. Sleeping's okay. Come on, Jerry, we're just leaving. No problem. Nothing wrong here."

"Nothing?" Nick said a bit louder.

"Yeah, nothing," Jerry offered walking backwards fast. The three turned and sprinted toward their truck.

"You're one bad ass motherfucker," Buddy said when Nick got back into the car. "Can we sleep now? You've shook up the whole lot."

"I don't think so," Nick said.

"So I'm not gonna quarrel with you, big Daddy. Just get some sleep. We deliver at nine sharp."

"I'm thinking of going back," Nick said.

Buddy straightened up, put his hands on the steering wheel, and then slumped a bit. He finally said, "Yeah, why not. After the delivery we're free for anything. Just some sleep now." He relaxed back into his tilted seat. "Just some sleep now."

"I can do most of the driving back," Nick said.

"We can solve that after the delivery. Just sleep now. We got keep rested."

"Yeah, rested," Nick said. "Rested for the trip back."

2.

At 9:15a.m. they were parked in a strip mall directly in front of Armstead Realty. Buddy said, "Okay, take the package in there, and give it to Bonnie. Only Bonnie. She'll ask you to wait while she opens it and makes sure everything's there."

"What is in it?" Nick asked.

"Don't know, something she wants. This is the third time I've delivered it. Probably a half hour and then we're off."

Nick got out of the car, opened the back door, and took up the brown papered box. It was lighter than he imagined. He looked back at Buddy when he pulled the glass door open, but Buddy waved him on in. Bonnie was in the third open cubicle on the right. She had the name Bonnie elaborately stenciled on the gray glass at the top of her partition. Nick liked the purple lettering. Even more he liked the rose cologne smell suffusing her chamber. She didn't notice him and eventually he tapped her splendidly soft right shoulder. "Package from Jersey," he said with some surprising jauntiness.

She took off her headphones and turned to him. "You're not Buddy," she said, smiling with Nick suspected/hoped was some approval.

"You wanna open it?" Nick asked, all apparent business while he watched her red tank top and scanned her strange lemon-colored rubber boots. She deftly produced a box cutter and severed the packing tape on the box and sliced through the central seam.

"You turn around," she said to Nick. "This is for my eyes only. You see that film?"

"Yes," Nick answered, suddenly picturing the nude women sliding through tan oil, and wondered if a well-suited fellow might point a gun at him someday.

"Yeah, it's all here. You and Buddy can take it to the lake." She snapped it shut and handed it back to Nick, who wanted to prolong the encounter but couldn't think of anything to say. He eased backward, smiling at her and finally turned toward the entrance. Buddy must have found a parking space. He walked back and forth looking for Buddy, checking the parking lot. After five minutes he went back inside.

"Buddy's gone," he said.

She took off her headphones again, swiveled to stare directly at him. She let her eyes survey him in a way he found strangely thrilling. After five seconds she finally said, "No shit! That bastard. That fucking bastard."

"Maybe he went on an errand," Nick said.

"You don't know Buddy, do you? He's left us the little fucking errand, hasn't he?"

"Errand?" Nick asked.

"Yeah, that bastard. Now we'll have to take it to the lake. Buddy doesn't like to get his tootsies wet."

"What does that mean?"

"He's a fucking coward, every third delivery has to go to the lake and every time he finds a way out of it. I bet he's halfway back to Jersey. Fucking coward. Somebody somewhere told him there's alligators around the lake and suddenly he's one scared little boy, and mommy has to pick up the pieces."

"Mommy?" Nick said.

"Figure of fucking speech," she answered. "Look," she fumbled in her pocketbook at the side of the castered chair. She pulled out a set of keys. "Around the side lot," she motioned to her right, "a blue Camaro, bring it to the front and we'll make the fucking delivery.." She tossed him the keys and smiled in a way that convinced him. A blue Camaro, a blonde in lemon rubber boots and alligators in an empty swamp. Golden sunlight and sea, and possibility swelling within him.

"Get out, I'm driving." She said when he brought the car around.

Soon enough they were out into Florida's sunbaked flatland.

"Where's the lake?" Nick asked as they passed onto Grovernor Boulevard."

"Okeechobee," she answered. "An hour and a half away, if we're lucky."

"I guess we're lucky," Nick answered.

"Maybe Buddy's always the lucky one." She said. "How'd you meet him?"

"My bus broke down in New Jersey. He worked where I spent the night. I don't know him."

"So, you decided to take a long car trip with him?" she asked, smiling.

"It seemed like the best idea."

"Because you had to get out of New Jersey, is that it?"

"Maybe."

"I guess you like driving with strangers."

"I like driving with you."

"Are you coming on to me?"

"Yes, of course!"

Her reaction was disarmingly automatic and intoxicating, "Well, we gotta make the delivery first."

"I can wait," Nick instantly said.

"I like that," she answered, and reached over patting his left knee.

Nick closed his eyes, and consciously breathed slowly. She left her hand in place. So it was as in Hollywood films, Nick thought, easy women who understood his ravenous need, and matched his every step in imagined ascent to perfect lust. Together they would scramble to ecstasy, again and again, probing each other's body to release wet torrents of blinding affection. On the big screen of his mind her sleek slopes of flesh folded into him over and over. Trampoline hillocks of thigh, stomach, breasts for his treasured stomping; suckingly toward release.

The Motel Six's room "used and therefore reduced in price" was slightly off target of his vision. The air in the long-sealed room was thick with past occupant odor, full of particulates churning as they both churned on the sagging bed. Maybe the previous occupant slept beside a dog or maybe an incontinent cat, Nick thought when the initial knob of passion had spurted. But she was hardly done. Her legs twined with his, and her hand in his crotch slowly stroked, clutched, enmeshed, and coached him to a greater erection that she slowly steered into her. With each coaching she kissed him deeply letting her tongue play across his gums and the aching roof of his mouth. "Yes, you can. Yes, you must," she pulled back enough to say in spurts of hot breath.

"Yes!" she sighed egging him deeper and more passionately into her. His vision swam furiously toward a lush fusion of Rita Hayworth and Jennifer Lawrence in the films that had most entranced him in Samoa: *Gilda* and *American Hustle*. So these American women knew passion unbounded, untapped, unbridled. He must study and run toward their joy. He must crush all hesitancy. This one reached inside of him to unspool his intestines to dump out his essence in the sagging cave of failing steel springs and paper-thin foam rubber topping.

Eventually she prodded him out of total collapse. "We still have time," she whispered. "I can take you higher, wider, fuller, emptier. Yes, emptier. We can empty ourselves."

"Stop!" he murmured sluggishly, then used a phrase he'd heard from American sailors outside Tutuila, "My nuts feel like two raisins in a shopping bag."

"What?" she laughed. "You never heard that in New Delhi."

"You think I'm Indian?"

"I don't care what you are. I want more of you." She answered. "And we've got time."

3.

Violent thunder and a near horizontal rain lambasting the ancient Jalousie windows of their room awakened him. She was sitting in the lone armchair which she had turned toward the pale small T.V. Home drama, he sensed, was playing on the screen and there were periodic shouts and murmurings. Bonnie was smoking a sloppily rolled cigarette.

"Not bad," she said turning to him. "Not hash, but not bad. Want a hit?"

He waved her off.

"Such a good boy," she said.

"Yes, I'm good boy," Nick said. "A good and happy boy."

She laughed and got up from the chair. She held the cigarette close to his lips, "Take a hit. It'll restore you."

"Re . . . Store." Nick echoed then drew a long toke. "Okay, let's get married."

"What?" she said, turning back to the T.V.

"We should get married, right now."

"Are you of the fellas who get laid and think marriage is part of it?"

"My father said I'd know when it comes time to marry, and now I know. It's just as he said. And I know now. Now I know."

"Can we take a shower first?"

"Only if you say yes, first."

"Well, I'm saying *yes* to a shower. That's what I'm saying *yes* to."

"No. I'm serious. Say yes to marriage right now." He got out of bed and appeared taller than she remembered. Naked and taller, and darker. Bonnie felt a sudden fear sweep into her. There was apparent hostility in his tone and stance and suddenly she began to think it might be time to accept his invitation upon pain of some dreadful consequence. Perhaps time to acquiesce in order to gain time to resist or escape later.

"Okay, I accept," she said with a small giggle. But he grabbed her left shoulder, squeezing with such intensity that she felt pain down her side, well into her leg and left knee.

"Mean it!" he said not releasing his grip.

"Of course, I mean it. Can't you see I'm all putty in your hands? Now let's get washed off and maybe try another round."

He released her, kept the cigarette, and sat in the chair before the T.V. She hurried to the bathroom, imagining Nick had turned into Robin Williams in The Photographer or maybe Jake Gyllenhaal in Nightcrawler. It would take some guile to be rid of him.

From the bathroom she called Buddy, already on the road back to New Jersey. He supplied her the name of co-owner of a dinner at the Southwest corner of Lake Okeechobee—a fellow who sometimes pretended to be a County Sherriff in order to shake down rival drug dealers. Buddy was sure he'd delight in acting as a marriage official, for a simple two hundred dollars. For an additional fifty Buddy agreed to set it up.

After her bath Bonnie became impatient to go ahead with the sham marriage, imagining that Nick in marital ecstasy would not stop her from slipping away. It was, she understood, a very clumsy rouse, but it had a certain comic whimsy that she instinctively believed could actually, should actually, work. The sheriff, she explained to Nick, was waiting for them, having cancelled for the day his work of shutting down massage parlors attached to a trailer park at the lake's most southern inlet. She laughingly suggested for their projected Honeymoon they might try a three or foursome at the "Bide-Awhile Yoga Temple."

"Be serious, "Nick said to her. "This is a significant step."

"Oh, baby, I am serious. Let's dress up for the occasion. I'll get an iron from the front desk and press your shirt."

At 6:20 p.m. they arrived at Vic's Lakeside Diner, and Russ Beamer came out to greet them in his pressed grey Sheriff's shirt with an arrow patch over the left front pocket. "The happy couple!" he shouted. Handshakes all around. "There are papers to be signed, just formal county records stuff, very similar to subpoenas, a lot of legal mumbo jumbo. And I will have to see some ID's."

Beamer easily dismissed Bonnie's driver's license, but paused over Nick's ID. "Heh, armed forces green card. Never seen one of those. But good enough. Bonnie said she wanted the crisp and clear briefest one allowable. There are several, you know. But I like this concise, precise set of promises, overseen by my office and stamped with my signature. When I finish you may kiss the bride." Beamer laughed loudly. "We can do it out back since there are customers in the diner. It's a nifty view of the lake—biggest self-contained east of the Mississippi."

When the lake came into view Nick smiled and suddenly imagined it was an off shoot of Vatic Bay. He wanted his father there beside him, maybe bouncing anxiously up and down in his orange flip flops, perhaps humming some Samoan chant full of constrained enchantment.

When the vows were finished Nick kissed Bonnie and held on longer than she wanted. Then he turned and suddenly went into the diner and announced to an elderly couple in the first booth.

"I just got married. I just got married in America!"

Beamer pulled Bonnie near to him and whispered: "Your stud sports dog tags . . ."

"What's that mean?" Bonnie asked.

"He's in the Army for God's sake. So what's he doing here? On liberty or AWOL? That's absent without leave. I notify his Coast Guard base and they'll pick him up."

"How quickly?" Bonnie asked.

"CG's Lifeboat Station is about half hour away."

"That's great! Notify them."

"Ah, true love." Beamer said.

"True additional insurance," Bonnie added, "I don't see him again."

"Marriage changes everything, don't it?" he smiled, then added, "Just funnin' ya. I'll call Griffiths now. They'll pick him up before too long, especially if I keep him here."

"You keep him here. I'm gone, way gone."

"Gone where, little vixen?"

"I don't know, maybe St. Louis. Maybe further west. Keep him here."

"I know why you're lying to me. I get it. No problem looks like he loves the diner. And I'll offer him a marriage feast."

"And you'll think of something to tell him."

"Of course. I'm a good storyteller—maybe something about the Seminoles hereabouts. Maybe his people? Didn't they get marched to Oklahoma?"

"You'd know better than me," Bonnie said, sidling by the diner windows to reach her car.

4.

"She got a call from her sick mama. Had to leave immediately. She'll meet you back at the motel later tonight. She's sorry and loves you very much. She'll make it up to you," Beamer smiled at Nick and patted his own crotch, nodded and winked.

Nick seemed amazed and instinctively stepped back, colliding with the stools lining the dinner's counter. "Later tonight?" he finally asked.

"You bet. She's really sorry, being it your marriage day and all, but her mama maybe comes first. And that just might be an ongoing problem for you. Not that I'm in the business of giving free marital counseling. But if I were you, I'd play it just the way she wants. You wait for her at the motel and then you fly way away together. You'd better do that, don't you think? You being AWOL and all. You shouldn't let folks see those dog tags, you know. People will ask questions, maybe make phone calls and then you'll get returned. I'm assuming you don't want that, do you? I'll tell ya what. I'll drive you back to the motel, but first let's get Ellie to push out a veritable marriage feast for you. You can eat for two, and for me of course." Beamer pushed through and took a stool. "You sit next to me, and I'll tell ya how women act some time. I've had a lot experience with Bonnies in my time." He pulled Nick onto the adjacent stool, and then shouted to the hefty woman in a white nurse's uniform behind the counter, "Ellie, Ellie, time to break out your best steak and fries for Nick and me. It's wedding celebration time. You know that best beef from Japan. Whadya call it? Kobeee something or other. The best meat, Ellie. Nick here's a young fellow, needs to keep his strength up. Don't ya, Nick? Don't ya? Nick! Are you listening to me? Listen up! I'll drive ya back to the motel. In four more hours, she come back, and you'll forget about this meal, this diner, this sheriff. I promise ya, Nick, I promise ya."

Nick seemed to slump down over his stool. He put his elbows on the counter to stop his body from dribbling down to the wide pine board floor, apparently freshly polyurethaned. Finally he said, quietly, "Her mama? Her mama?"

"I said that," Beamer answered. "Don't worry about that. She'll fix things. She was in a terrible rush. Something emergency. You get it? Emergency room some place, on the other end of the lake. Nothing too serious, but serious enough, she had to rush off. She said, tell Nick I'm sorry. I'll meet him back at the motel later tonight. Tonight. Got it? Tonight. Just hours from now." Beamer stopped and pushed away the salad plate Ellie had slid onto the countertop. "I don't eat salads," he said to Nick quietly. "And she knows that all too well. Means she doesn't like what I'm saying, but it's the truth. Bonnie will meet you later. I think much later, but she'll be coming back to the motel sometime later tonight. You can count on that. But more important than that is where you'll go next. Ya gotta think hard about that. You're on the run, aren't you?" Beamer stopped and looked at Nick. "Aren't you?"

Nick suddenly saw Gabbon's puzzling smile. His almost genuflective hostile behavior, awaiting Bosunmate Moulton's summons, or maybe just a moment when Nick stopped guarding his own back . . . . For that moment Nick imagined a double- handed thrust would topple the sheriff across the tops of stools to his right and he might strike his head on any of them, but would that make Bonnie reappear? Why not try that? He swiveled to the right, tightened his core, and finally muttered, "I want Bonnie back."

"So do I and when we get to the motel maybe she'll already be there. Her mama don't live that far from here. Now eat your steak. It's the best damn beef in Florida and that's sayin' something!"

"I want Bonnie," Nick said it quietly, picking up his flimsy, saw-toothed steak knife. He wondered if it might bend or snap if he plunged it into Beamer's soft left belly. And he was genuinely surprised when it went straight in, neither bending nor snapping.

"Jesus!" Beamer howled. "What the fuck? Why?"

Nick twisted the knife to stop Beamer from groaning and complaining.

"Jesus! No! For God's sake no!" he jumped to the right, ramming his back into the next stool and slumping slowly down between them.

Nick delayed that fall by grabbing the right flap pocket of Beamer's mock sheriff's jacket, ripping car keys out, as Beamer fell.

Part III

Containment and Asymmetrical Warfare

Chapter Eight

Putting the statement on her desktop, Solomon Sears acknowledged to his wife Ava, "You said you were pretty sure I would be allowed some kind of opening remarks, so I've made some notes about how I'd proceed."

"I said Dillon was pretty flexible, but I also said Grand Juries didn't allow lengthy pontifications, little hymns to your own expertise. Doesn't look from the length of this you paid much attention to what I said."

Sears thought about taking the pages back, but finally said, "I'm always anxious to get editing. Lots can be axed, if necessary."

"*Necessary* seems always one of your retreat words, just before you curl up under an afghan and scream 'in-coming!'." Ava laughed.

"Could you just take a look at it?"

"Why?"

"You have the experience in these adventures. I'm a lowly academic unfamiliar with the lethality of the legal world. I'd value your protection."

"Oh, Mommy, don't get out your silver hairbrush again. Solly doesn't want a spanking."

"Just read through and make some cuts."

"Spank, spank! Spank! For God's sake, Solly, stop moaning. Develop a little spine."

"Notes for an impending deposition"

Perhaps opening statement: "I first met the Hassan brothers when they enrolled in my History of 20th Century American Foreign Policy, when that title still seemed inclusive (I suppose that little fillip might lead to distracting discussion of why two decades of the 21st century have been omitted from the course's title. With luck we could spend perhaps ten minutes belaboring that issue. And my astute lawyers told me anything that eats into deposition time is worth doing, which makes me wonder how much time they've spent taking depositions. Not much I fear, but then for their wages one cannot complain, at least not till complaining additionally drags out the process.) Ava glanced up from the text and said, "Get to the point."

I found the Hassan brothers fascinating, intellectually and visually. Mahmoud the older, and much taller one was heavily bearded, had a softly thick voice tone that simultaneously seemed ingratiating and concerned, interested in hearing what you had to say. His brother Saif lived up to that name, (he told me it meant 'sword of justice') smaller, compact, energetic with a kind of scowling fierceness and focus that seemed intent not on listening to you but rather toward messing you up, startling you, knocking you off balance and then figuratively shoving you over a cliff. Saif, as everyone called him, was beardless, with narrow eyes constantly darting above and around you. He spoke in a beguiling conspiratorial whisper, as if every word both of us exchanged was being recorded somewhere he knew, but I didn't. He was shorter than his brother and seemed far meaner. I wondered how they related to each other. Saif after any particular lecture would approach me with objections to my presentation. He often reminded me that it seemed I lacked appreciation for the majesty of Arab intellectual life over centuries, and I of course failed to see how Islam permeated every aspect of existence in the Middle East and North Africa, to say nothing of Southeast Asia.

Ava noted "Self-serving dicta, they already know you're an expert, don't they? The point is to convince everyone that you are both trustable and likeable. Got it?"

Mahmoud never spoke of politics. He would, however, usually nod when his feisty brother made some derogatory remark about Al-Sisi and Egyptian politics. It was my innocent question about such politics that led to Saif's lengthy presentation of the sins of the Egyptian regime. What I knew about Egypt would rattle in a thimble, and Saif soon delighted in filling in my picture. Mahmoud on the other hand was a serious scuba diver and rather than lecture me on Egyptian politics would several times knock on the front door and present us with a chill bag of large sea scallops, the very best I've ever eaten and doubtless best I ever will—the kind of scallops that sell for over 18 bucks per pound. And in restaurants more than that if you can find it. Only the pitifully little bay scallops, a synonym for skate or cod simply punched out in quarter sizes sans lady liberty on either side. Yes, I get it. No jokes in a deposition. Nothing even remotely funny about *The Incident*. But I want to emphasize what Attorney Dillon has said, namely, that I know absolutely nothing about *The Incident*.

And because I don't know anything about *The Incident* I understand I'm here only to reveal Saif's state of mind, his state of intention just prior to *The Incident*. Is that the case? Have I understood why I'm here? Is that really the case? I can tell you a great deal about Saif's ideology, a great deal about his understanding of American foreign policy, America's quest in the world. I can fill in those blanks and I suppose you can use that information to construct your own understanding of *The Incident.* Is that correct? I understand I'm not here to ask you questions. But you need to understand something before I fill you in. I consider it crucial to understanding Saif.

Ava noted, "Too emphatic. Never insult a Grand Jury by asserting you know more than they could know. Never! as much as it's your standard operating procedure. For example we've talked about you constantly interrupting me."

"They want my testimony, not my conversion." Sears said. "I'll go ahead as if that was a sidebar to my witnessing."

"They'll know erasure when they see it practiced automatically and unthinkingly."

Sears paused, nodded, caught often between recognizing his wife's humor and retreating before her hectoring. Sears decided it was better to burrow on to find a seal-slick statement before the jury. He finally remarked, although it hurt, "To return to the matter at hand."

You need to grasp Saif's and Mahmoud's commitment to Islam. Let me tell you one illustrative story, because it might color how you think about everything I tell you. At the university I became the first and only faculty advisor of the new club Saif and Mahmoud created, *The Muslim Student Association.*

"First and foremost, how typical! And completely irrelevant to persuading the jurors that you have anything worth listening to."

"So, you presume to know what they know or need to know."

"I presume to have conducted a hundred more depositions before a Grand Jury than you have done even one. And I'm not even going to bill you."

"God, I'm so lucky we're married."

I know later it had some affiliation with the infamous Muslim Brotherhood, but initially it was just one of the many university clubs providing an opportunity for like- minded students to enjoy each other's company and values.

Ava interrupts, "Maybe I should offer an aside— something along the lines that you are, charitably put, a self-regarding person much more at home pontificating, attempting and usually failing, to impress whatever audience you're before. That might make you more likeable, a veritable Hillary Clinton among the deplorables."

Sears looked sourly at Ava, "I don't think that would help much. Let me go on. Soon enough they'll see what a sweet fellow I am."

"Sweet and narcissistic."

To continue: Maybe the MSA kids wanted to study the Koran together, although I suspect it was more in line with Mahmoud's focus—just social interaction, mutual support in an alien environment. Maybe a way for the boys to get together with the girls in some strangely sanctioned way. I couldn't tell. Just a way of being Muslim together in a world that didn't grasp or appreciate Islam. Have you ever lived in an alien culture? It's quite revealing—knocks your paradigms on their ass. Tosses your assumptions in the veritable pit.

"Good God! Now you're offering therapy to the jury. You're preaching cross-culturalism to them. They'll dismiss everything you say."

Anyway, I told the brothers I was willing to sign on as their faculty advisor of this new club, but only if they would supply me with a new Koran in English, so I could learn a little about their guiding religion. They nodded to this request and I signed the club document. Is that why I'm called here now? Because I signed up to be their advisor on their new club, perhaps the only faculty member willing to do so, out of a commitment to letting a thousand flowers bloom at this university, in line with its widely celebrated principles. Is that why I'm called here now to tell you all I know about their state of mind when they first came here?

I apologize for discursiveness, but the important point I'm making is that despite my request no Koran appeared either in my office mailbox or at my office, in spite of several related meetings with both of them. Two months went by then three, at least three official meetings of the club at which each time I was introduced as the faculty advisor. Still no Koran. Still Prof.Sears left in the dark about the elements he allegedly advised. I knew of course lots of faculty advisors existed in name and signature only, but that was not my commitment, my intention. My intention was to know something about the club I was advising, and its allegedly founding document the sacred Koran. But no copy was forthcoming. So finally, I asked Saif and Mahmoud what had I missed? Why after repeated requests did no Koran land on my desk? Was it too expensive? They immediately laughed and too loudly. "You don't understand what we believe," Saif said, still chuckling at my what he labelled as my "very American obsession" with expense. I agreed and reemphasized I needed the Koran to understand thoroughly what they believed. Mahmoud interrupted, "We believe, if we directly hand you the Koran and you don't accept Islam, as we're convinced you won't, then we believe you'll be condemned to eternal hellfire. So we'll never do that."

I thought, "Henh! Real belief. I've not run into that before, at least not at the university. "So you want me to get my own Koran and slip out of hellfire from you all."

"I doubt you'll escape," Saif said.

"But at least you'll be blameless," I countered.

"Distant causation," Saif muttered.

What's important is that I got a brief glimpse where they were coming from. It jerked me up a bit. But there's a kicker in the story. A couple of weeks later a very lithe Muslim woman, probably a grad student who I'd seen at the club meetings, walked into my office unannounced and put a mint copy in English of the complete Koran on my desk. She smiled as if to say it was okay with her if that meant I went straight to hell. She half nodded and walked directly away. I spent a good bit of time reading the text, but it's pretty discursive, boring, repetitive, and just weird—I've learned subsequently that it only makes sense if you read it in Arabic, which I have no intention of doing, ever. But that can't really be true, since so much of the Muslim world doesn't read Arabic but still embraces the Koran. Yes, I know the preferred spelling nowadays is "Qur'an", but Koran says it better. My own little Pinyin-like assertion."

"Ah, more instruction. The little pontificator never misses a chance. Get rid of it."

The only point is that everything the Hassans do is conditioned by their grasp of Islam. Everything. We can't understand them if we don't enter their universe, their Caliph-driven dreams, their understanding of how the world works, how aliens must inevitably treat them.

Now I know that since the incident, the world wants to know everything about the Arabs in my Carriage House. The Arabs in my Carriage House. I've been confused for Arabs. I have indeed. When Ava and I were living in Yamada outside of Osaka in the 70's (such a long time ago) we had dinner one night in a nifty complex of shops in Senri Chuo, a popular gathering spot for suburban Osaka-ites and we finished and stood in a taxi queue and swiftly enough (Japan is always efficient) got into a cab and the driver drove off without a word. Ava shut me down and said, "Let see if he knows where we live." "He apparently does," I whispered in reply. And he continued to drive going up on a highway and presently took us to a mammoth apartment complex near Minami Senri's train station. He stopped, opened the back door, using the lever release near his right knee, and said in loud and carefully rehearsed English, "Home at last!" But of course it wasn't our home, it was the home of some Arabs we'd met at the American Center in Osaka. In Japan all foreigners look alike, just like Japanese look alike to us. I tell you these things because it's a complicated game grasping an alien brain.

Of course I can tell you how Saif in particular judged American actions abroad and American values in the homeland. But it's not a reassuring picture. You won't like his diagnosis. He didn't like it much either. He seemed always anxious to prod me to gin up a refutation of his fevered interpretation. I could easily provide the standard denials—of course America was only interested in spreading democracy and justice, equality and a democratically run (capitalist fed) world safe always for infinite tolerance of the great globe's diversity. I could goad him into fierce eloquence concerning our alleged sins. We'd intervened so that Kuwait could continue to exploit Pakistani and Bangladeshi workers doing the dirtiest work Kuwait could generate. And of there were the murderous coups the CIA hatched installing the appalling dictatorships throughout the Middle East. Remember old Mossadegh, sacrificed for the American sanctioned Shah.

And how we bolstered both Iran and Iraq so long as they killed each other. We supplied with cash and weapons whatever mutual slaughter we could encourage in the Middle East. How else look at our "presence" in Yemen? Our intrusions into Libya and Egypt, Sudan. Our special forces were everywhere. Constant trouble. The litany grew tiresome, as tiresome as Mahmoud's nodding ascent.

If you need me to buttress a shaky case concerning Saif's "intentions" regarding *The Incident*, then I'm your lad all right. He was filled with righteous, bilious hatred for these United States, and with reason given our nasty proclivity to spread violence and butchery wherever we go. Is that you want from me? Or should I tame it down with phrases like "national interest" and "realist foreign policy" "balance of power" "group think" "inherent bad faith model" and on and on. It seemed to me then and now that we showered each other with mirror fake assertions, fake not quite news. It was, and is, a way to keep Maginot Lines shored up, solid in their mutual absurdity. Whoever wants to get beyond their hatred?

So why, then, did you rent them your carriage house? Rent? Not quite accurate . . . not quite accurate. I didn't rent them the carriage house. The pandemic did, old Covid did. Old Covid preached eloquently the mutual dependence we wouldn't have wanted to expose. It was our gesture, Ava's, and mine, to our common humanity and our imagined tax write off had not the law been so savagely changed. Besides, had we gone to the usual parties we would have delighted in dropping in near-whispers the sentence, "There are Arabs in our carriage house."

Think of the gracious reverberations all over George-town. Besides, Ava's minders in The Company always intoned it was essential to keep our enemies closer than our friends. What could be closer than the Carriage House? Perhaps our bedroom, Sears thought, beginning to imagine Ava amid the perfume the brothers seemed always to wear. The four of them in the Queen size bed and muttering Allah Akbar . . . . It's a shame they weren't more attractive. Mahmoud always had a briny scent as if he'd just slipped out of his wetsuit. And Saif had an angry smoky cast as if he had just finished a cigarette outside someplace but the burnt scent lingered on his shirt and sweater vests. But that reality was daily buried in an acrid Gardenia scent, tinged distantly with Rose sweetness, as if just slapped on before the walk over to the main house.

"He was on the cusp of assassination," Ava said. "Locked and loaded," she added now "and take out 'minders and the company.' Adds nothing and is dangerous to me, Solly. You wouldn't want to get us firebombed, would you?"

"Don't be ridiculous," Sears answered. "He's right here in front of us. We know him. It's inconceivable. You've swum too long in the paranoid sea. His innate gentleness makes it unthinkable."

"You're really quite afraid of this Grand Jury, aren't you?"

"Scared to death," Sears said slowly. "What if Dillon starts quoting some of my unpatriotic prose. What if he suggests I poisoned Saif's thinking? What if he gets me to admit Saif's correct?"

"But he is our acolyte, isn't he? Our carriage-hot-house would-be pool boy."

"Jesus! Could that all come out too?"

"Not so long as I draw breath and have access to Novichok." Ava laughed. "The really important thing is that you absolutely steadfastly stay away from *The Incident*. It has no connection to you. You know nothing of it. He and his brother lived as model tenants on your property, but they never discussed anything with you except adjustments to the rent or delays. No. Actually that's a damn rabbit hole. Don't go there. Dillon will be relentless. You never talked to the boys about anything except the weather. Answer only in monosyllables. Simply yes, or simply no. No elaboration. No explanation. Volunteer nothing. Whatever you or I did with the boys has nothing to do with *The Incident*. Nothing. Absolutely no relevance."

"Boys?"

"The maternal invocation. Works every time. Care devastates conspiracy. Don't worry. We looked after them with compassion and out of knowledge of what it means to be alien in a different culture. We knew from the inside what refugees face."

"Really?"

"Get a grip, Solly. I'm telling you things to hold in mind so that they condition how you speak. Nothing more. If you know the backstory cold, the front story never goes off the rails."

"And what if the back story is sick, diseased? What then?"

"So, we take the Novichok. And it all works out perfectly."

"I wish I had your insouciance."

"If you did, believe me I'd feel better too. You need steadying and more rehearsal. I'll play Dillon, and you can sharpen and shorten, really shorten, your answers."

"I've got a better idea."

"What?"

"I make mojitos and you get to be Dillon after dinner."

"Excellent! And then we'll have the Hassans over again, for naked, so to speak, political discussions." Ava laughed again and faked doubling over with mirth.

Sears said, "I'll try another draft."

2.

By the third mojito Solly had begun to enjoy the mint scent from the crushed leaves against the narrow tall glass's deliberately thick walls. The wooden muddler literally filled the space so that mashing the mint was almost automatic; simply turning the dowel mutilated the fresh leaves without much pressure needed. And the crushed petals slid down the sides of the glass and accumulated at the bottom for further, unplanned pressing. Solly took smiling relaxed delight in the incessant tapping mangling of the mint shards. He added to each glass yet another quarter inch of rum beyond his own earnestly celebrated recipe. Each rum increment raised, he believed, the possibility of taking the game they played with the Hassan brothers several notches deeper into potential ecstasy and irony.

"I'm adding ounces so we can explore Abu Ghraib more and more thoroughly." He said to Ava, who slowly stroked the full package of linguini fini into the boiling salt-flaked water. Solly in three long gulps tossed off his first Mojito.

"Don't get too head a start," Ava said watching him muddle a second drink.

"You notice how muddling almost duplicates the sound of a head banging into a thin wall?" Solly asked.

"How far do want to take our Abu Ghraib? Do we get to kill Mahmoud?"

"I'm interested in your choice," Solly said. "Not Saif, but Mahmoud. I'll drink to that."

"Nobody's dying, except in the Elizabethan sense of that lovely word." Ava said.

"Such a poet. Such a poet . . ." Solly said.

"Mahmoud's the real threat, Ava continued. "The quiet ones. Saif's too interested in arguing, getting the details right, making sure domination is convincingly based, although I noticed when he gets naked, his argument wilts." She chuckled.

"He responds best to dog collar and leash." Solly laughed. "Don't we all?" And he muddled himself a third drink.

"Be careful. Drink too much and you'll miss the best part." Ava said.

"The best part," Solly said reflectively. "The best, part maybe is sitting on the veranda and waiting to take our Lariam every Sunday afternoon, feeling the cooling breeze down the Victorian lanes of our hill station town. Listening to the breeze and hearing the padded feet of the various attendants meeting our needs, our wants. On the hottest days simply waving slow fans near us to simulate assuring wind, comforting, soothing, softly stroking wind."

"A lot of soft stroking. You and Dillon making a naked bench for Mahmoud to climb on, setting up naked Saif for the sheet I threw over him, standing like a tented crucifixion, arms outstretched, leash still attached to his collar, so I could tug the whole pig pile down. And which I never could do since you insisted on videoing everything and the auto click never seemed to work."

"And why did you invite Dillon in?"

"Ah, Solly, you know perfectly well. To compromise him, surely you see that."

"I do not."

"More importantly. He's not coming tonight. Our spontaneous game excludes Dillon per force."

"Good!" Solly shouted, "Now summon the lads to the prison pig pile."

"We'll eat first. I'm not getting them in here to watch us eat."

"Maybe we should skip the meal. I'm getting excited." Solly said.

"Always premature," Ava sighed.

Sullen in that rebuke, Solly responded, "I'll direct them to the cellar in, what shall we say, half an hour?"

"Oh, in deference to your needs, say, fifteen minutes." Ava answered.

The pasta was consumed al dente, and the meal ended with diced crabapples sprinkled with cinnamon sugar, Solly and Ava hurried down the heavily treaded steps to the cellar game room.

Mahmoud, sopping wet in a Speedo, was already settled into the giant faux leather recliner. "No Dillon tonight?" he asked.

"No Dillon. No bench tonight. Maybe only a fierce beating—flogging," Ava said.

"I'll get the leashes, oh, colonial dominatrix," Saif playfully exclaimed. "Make me pay for my rebellious longing." He dropped his sweatpants and kicked them away with his flip flops deep under the billiard table. He started to unbutton his shirt when a ferocious knocking, evidently from the front door upstairs, suddenly brought the room out of its sandstorm of swelling lust to an embarrassingly normal linoleum-floored, poorly lit, mucid space of tiredness and the evening news on an invisible, unheard television.

Part IV

Mutual Assured Destruction

Chapter Nine

"Good Christ!" Solly shouted and turned heading back up the steps.

"ICE?" Mahmoud asked, apparently genuinely terrified, as he bolted from the chair and out through the open sliding glass doors, into the back yard and running toward the carriage house.

"Of course not!" Ava shouted, but that did not slow his exit.

Saif dropped the leashes, and crouched, then lay to yank his pants from beneath the table. He pulled them on and began re-buttoning his shirt.

Ava held up her hand, slowing Saif. "Probably just a neighbor," she said, straining to hear what Solly might be encountering. "No need to end the game, just yet."

"I'm losing my conviction," Saif answered, smiling. "ICE is everywhere, aren't they?"

"Not in this part of Georgetown," Ava said, moving back up the steps and sensing that Solly had taken on the pompous tone of Professor Sears, and that meant students or subordinates were involved, and that meant her fixed vision of Mahmoud, nearly naked in the lounge chair, faded to his scared sprint to carriage house. Total, collapse of the Abu Ghraib game. A wilted termination. She'd found Saif too energetic and quick and begun to fantasize Mahmoud as the lover of slow delicious techniques.

Now she could hear Prof. Sears saying, "Now Creighton. Now Creighton. I can understand your fears and hers too. I can understand that, but I'm not at all sure I can solve your dilemma."

"It's just a night or two," Creighton was whining. "Just till the seminar concludes. We can't stay in our hotel room. And --"

"Why not? You surely had a reservation for the whole length of the seminar." Sears interrupted him.

"The tragedy upended everything. And Bonnie's ex-husband is threatening us."

"About what?"

"About. . . . about . . . the accident, about his daughter's death. And my daughter's death."

"He's threatening you?"

"That's what he said," the woman with Creighton repeated. "And that's the truth, too. The God's honest truth, whether you believe it or not."

"I'm sorry," Creighton said, "this is Bonnie. The other mother." Creighton suddenly thought the phrase lingered in the evening air, *the other mother.* What could that mean? To cover Creighton said, "It's only for a night or two, till we get things sorted out."

Ava came through the dining room, setting the door swinging with energy. "Two deaths to sort out. That might take more than a night or two. I'm so sorry we'd have come sooner but we were downstairs for a nightly session educating a couple of Arab students staying in our carriage house.

How to live in America? Native customs and slang, that sort of thing. Part of the rental contract." Ava emphasized rental.

"We're not interested in a contract," Bonnie said hurriedly. "Just some place to stay tonight that doesn't require a credit card. We charge anything and Nick will find us."

"Well then, I'm sorry I don't know your name. I'm Ava."

"I'm Bonnie, just Bonnie."

"Just Bonnie . . . and hunted by Nick. Sounds intriguing. Tell me about Nick."

"He's an animal, a killer." Bonnie said, staring into Ava's eyes, then flashing a pleading look at Sears. "I mean he could be. He's mean enough."

"Aren't we all?" Ava said. "I don't have to keep saying that to our Arab tenants, do we Solly? They fill us in daily with their Muslim Brotherhood trash recitations. Stay with us a while and they'll fill you in with America's global sins, the terrible savagery in the American heart."

Creighton said, "We're not political. Way beyond that. Way beyond." By asserting so Creighton suddenly felt liberated, almost to the point he felt blimp-like, lifted above the cares of tenancy or worry about a night's lodging. He briefly wondered if he might in fact be circling above Tangiers. Where exactly was Tangiers? He remembered reading an account of two young Americans in Tangiers, living in a double wide and dressing like Arab servants in white flowing sheets. "Of course they're Americans," someone said in Creighton's memory. "Of course," he thought. In a trailer awaiting their fate. Aware that they had crossed some marker of decency and were hiding out in a cloud of hashish.

"I suppose we could put you up over the garage, my son's old room with a very trashy bath. There's a stairway to it from the kitchen." Ava said with a kind of sinister courtesy that amazed Solly. He wondered if she thought of them as recruits in a widened game of Abu Ghraib. What roles did she have in mind?

"They might be happier in a hotel nearby," Solly said, testing Ava's commitment.

"Nonsense," Ava answered. "Arabs in the carriage house and Nick victims over the garage. It makes perfect sense, doesn't it? We're a deserving refuge, aren't we? We care for the homeless and God himself helps us safely through the eye of the needle, doesn't he?"

"It was an actual place, a rock carving near the Damascus Gate, and you could go through it, by squeezing. You really could, so all that American alarm about excessive wealth is misplaced." Saif said, reappearing in slightly sloppy reassembly through the swinging door to the dining room.

Creighton imagined Saif in tented white cloth on a jagged cliff in Tangiers. Beneath his wind- whipped gown was there a hefty scimitar intended for Creighton's neck? I deserved it, Creighton thought. Yes, this khaki clad lad was the perfect substitute for avenging Nick. You cannot strangle your child in bath foam and call it a baptism, can you, Creighton wondered? Why not? Had he not given Jenna over to a new life?

Bonnie said, "I'm sorry. I need to pee."

"So, micturition can serve double duty—relief and directions to your accommodations for the night," Solly said delightedly, and watching the disappointment flood into his wife's smiling face. "I'll aim you both to the garage apartment, with its own bath and walk-in shower. You'll love the privacy. The stairs are off the kitchen." And Solly held the swinging door open for them.

2.

When Bonnie came out of the bathroom adjacent to the open eves room above the garage, she found Creighton lying on the red bedspread over a twin bed crammed in the corner beneath the slanted roof. His left arm lay across his face blocking his eyes, and for a moment it seemed he was crying, so she asked, "You okay?"

"Is Sybil with you now?" Creighton answered.

"Come on now, don't start that shit."

"It's not shit. It's just a question. Is she with you and . . . and Jenna, where is she?"

"I'm tired of playing this game. It's silly. Fucked up silly. So cut it out."

"We can get them back. I'm sure of it. We just have to be crafty. Very crafty." Creighton half laughed. "Gimme another one."

Bonnie joined in the quiet laughing. "Yeah, one more daughter for the gentleman lying on the red cot."

"Not a cot, a full twin. See? Come and join me and gimme another one."

She took another yellow pill from the bottle she was carrying. "One more daughter for the distraught dad."

"We can get them back. Before Nick does."

"Don't mention him, will ya? My God don't mention him. He can't find us here, can he?"

"You said he could find anyone."

"Yeah, but not fucking here! Nobody could find us here."

"Maybe the Arab knows Nick. They look alike."

"Yeah, the black beard. He's hiding Jenna. I know it."

"I told ya, to knock off that shit. I'm tired of it. They're not coming back. We know that."

"Of course," Creighton said, put his arm back over his eyes. "They take the refuse on a barge to the middle of the Atlantic, the very middle of the Bermuda Triangle, and God sweeps under all the trash of this life. All the distractions. God pushes it deep in some trench at the bottom of the ocean."

"And Jenna and Sybil play with the brown one-eyed sea creatures and tell us with their laughter that all is forgiven," Bonnie said slowly. "So you stop mouthing off about it. About us. About what we did, since it's done, isn't it? Or do you keep thinking we can undo it?"

"Why can't we undo it? We don't really know if we did it. Wasted. How could we be sure it wasn't a stupid hysterical longing for some release that hatched it only in our minds? Without ever undertaking the actual act. I mean we couldn't have, could we? Could we?"

"Fuck off! Here's another yellow one. It'll ease your mind. It'll get you out of whatever locked compartment you're in." She flipped the pill on the red bedspread now over his waist and legs.

He rose up on his right elbow and fumbled with his left hand for the pill. He placed it slowly in his mouth and reached up to pull her down within the red coverlet, swiveling his waist enough to press against her falling form. "For God's sake," he heavily said to her descending ear, "make me forget it, will you? Won't you, now? Right now."

Her hand answered him by easing beneath the bedspread and grabbing softly at his groin. Her kneading signaled needing indeed as if they both knew such ministrations would submerge his sad conjurings. He imagined a blimp dragged a charred cartoon message across the grey-stained, slanting plywood hovering over them: **Jenna and Sybil are dead, but we aren't. They're gone, but we're here.**

Chapter Ten

After midnight Creighton awoke suddenly confronting Jenna's desperate form crying out to him, holding her arms out to him through eerily translucent darkened plastic sheeting. As his eyes adjusted to her form, abruptly the scene changed. He found himself braced against the slide's ladder as the darkened swirl lifted the slide and sent it spinning overhead with Creighton somehow attached to it, and Sybil screaming his name from above and Jenna collapsing into what appeared to be a small spinning boulder that morphed into a daschund howling as its innards poured slowly out. Jenna's face appeared in the spiraling intestines, screaming through the blood and splayed tendons, cartilages, veins. "Daddy! Please, Daddy, please, please."

Gasping, Creighton sat upright. His head thudded into the slanted plywood overhead. He nodded and gulped, hoping to find sufficient air, sufficient coolness to stay conscious. He half swallowed, half choked and finally flopped forward clutching his throat as if trying to open it to suck in the darkness, as if to find slivers of oxygen. He remembered reading that Covid dropped your oxygen levels so that you blacked out as your lungs seemed to catch fire. He waited for flame searing to start, but none came. An inner voice whispered, "I'm okay. I'm okay."

He tossed away the red bedspread and crawled out of the bed to middle of the room and slowly stood up. His T shirt and boxer shorts felt wet and clinging. He stumbled toward the bathroom light and eventually made his way down the stairs to the kitchen. He heard voices talking agitatedly somewhere below him. He made his way through the swinging door and crossed the dining room to reach the stairs down to the cellar. The voices got louder. He heard Ava's voice, he was certain, but the responding male voice sounded younger and muffled.

Creighton eased down the steps, and the muffling became clear. Ava on brilliant orange floor pillow was watching someone entirely tented over by a white sheet. That someone was standing on a green plastic fold-up ten inch stool.

The tented voice spoke with increasing passion. "Your lust for acquisition began from the very first moment—so much more you wanted land not religious freedom—religion meant escape from freedom. So you pushed aside land's obvious owners, forced them deeper into the interior or sped them toward the periphery. Chemical/biological as well as weapons-driven exploitation ransacked their resistance. Toss them small pox infested towels and blankets. Toss cholera to them. Your earliest ordinances were always focused on protecting property, securing ownership, dispossessing native occupants, who had made as far as you were concerned no improvements in all the years of their control of the land."

"Enough blathering, " Ava shouted. "Lift the sheet. Lift it now and reveal your vile nakedness."

Immediately his hands yanked the sheet up, dark hairy legs stood on the green plastic stool.

"Higher!" Ava shouted. "Step off the stool and kneel before me, now! You vile rodent. You naked vile rodent."

So it was Saif totally naked and smiling, half laughing as he knelt down on the maroon linoleum of the cellar floor. "You cannot escape the treachery of your inception. Via disease and dispossession of the native inhabitants of what you now think was always your land. Yet you knew the land was never yours. It always belonged to Allah. Your inception began with pillage, with pillage! Your invocation of justice was always premised on your power. Your technology wrote your law, your sacred Constitutional processes—nothing but the interests of the stronger."

"And who is stronger here in this sacred cavern?" Ava asked pulling on the clothesline that, it became evident was knotted to a rubber band around Saif's neck. "Lie down, dog," Ava shouted.

"My lying down cannot silence the voices of the natives you ravaged, nor the English or French or Spanish you bully-pushed or butchered out North and South. They had come for the fountain of youth and found the fount of death!"

"Turn over on your back, you vile dog. Face upwards toward me. So we can violate you properly." Ava said, "Is that you Solly?" she called out without turning toward the stairs. "If that's you, Solly, come piss on this dog. This turd of a human being, so vulnerable in our power."

"I'm Creighton. What's going on?"

Abruptly Saif got up, pulling the sheet in front of himself, "We re-enacting Abu Ghraib prison as the most emblematic of all moments of America's presence in Arab lands. Stay a while and you'll see me turn the tables on Ava Sears, reducing her to the subjugation her land had wrought on my own for two centuries at least. I'll get my brother to piss on her for your delight.

Such games do delight you, do they not? They speak such joy to the average American heart. Is it not so? Does not such despoliation warm your heart? Do you not sanction and celebrate lynchings, tire burnings of people, not those you pushed aside, condemned to reservations or simply devoured their houses and livelihoods, but rather those you had actually imported involuntarily for your endless exploitation? I'm talking of those slaves your blessed Constitution christened as 3/5's of a person, infinitely traded for at least twenty more years, and prescribed against any escape by the distinguished Congress you created. Is it not so?"

"I'm sorry," Creighton said. "I'm not much for games. I'm sorry."

"Atrocities worry you, is that it? Saif asked. "If so how can you continue to live here?"

"Ah, Creighton, don't listen to this boy. He's a polished liar. But really only interested in sex."

"Speak for yourself, Ava!" Saif shouted.

"I'm sorry," Creighton repeated more quietly.

"Banish sorrow! Come join us, get those wet undies off. My boy, what in God's name have you been doing?" Ava shouted.

Creighton turned on the stairs and started back up, but Solly was coming down. In a swift burst of thrust he toppled Creighton onto the cellar floor.

"Such a bully," Ava sighed. "Such a patriarchal bully. Jesus, such brutality."

"It's instinctive among Americans," Saif continued his tirade. "Instinctive. Just as the great D. H. Lawrence said. You people are instinctive savages, gifted killers. Bloody murderers. It's in your blood. In your brain circuitry."

"Fucking A!" Solly concurred.

"Get rid of those wet, stinking undies," Ava said.

"I just want to go back up to bed," Creighton said slowly getting to his feet.

"You had better join the game. Otherwise they'll rat you out to ICE." Saif half laughed. "They will indeed. So join the tribe. You won't believe the payoffs."

Creighton steadied himself by grabbing onto the right railing lining the cellar stairs. He muttered to himself, "Jenna, I'm coming. Jenna, I'm coming for you."

"Dump those stinking undies in the laundry room," Ava shouted. "Christine will handle them in the morning."

"He needs to join the tribe," Saif shouted. "He needs initiation. He needs to join us. We need him to be a part of our rituals, don't we? Isn't that how the club works? So come on back Mr. Creighton, Come on back down. There's only safety if you join us. Come on back. Turn back. He has to join the atrocity. He has to become part of it. You always insisted on that, Ava."

"You don't get to call her Ava," Solly said, shaking his head. "And get dressed. Get dressed. Fun's over. No more frolic tonight."

"You don't run the game," Saif insisted. "She runs the game. It's up to her. Or it's a triune governing mechanism—three branches checking on each other—Mahmoud and me and the rest of you. Separate branches that have to work together. Power controlled. Power divided against domination. The American way, is it not? Division stops at the water's edge, doesn't it?"

"What horseshit!" Ava added. "You've got it all bollixed up."

"My balls agree," Saif laughed. "Jesus, what dissatisfaction! Weren't we saving the world? Didn't they love and treasure us? We twice skunked the Germans. We stopped the Soviets cold. And cold contained them. And watched them die. We buried Asian resuscitation at least for a hundred and fifty years, and we kept the Arabs from gathering any strength. Don't you want to join our tribe, Mr. Creighton? Aren't you proud of who you are? So very proud of your home nation? Didn't you relish decimating enemies? Incinerating millions . . . join us for the frolic of your life. As a new member you get to wear the collar and rope, get to defecate in public, so to speak. Think of the joy of it. And, by the way, who the fuck is Jenna?"

"Enough! "Solly shouted, taking the nylon rope from Ava and yanking it savagely so that Saif was suddenly on his knees and soundless.

Thankful for the silence, Creighton quickly ran up the stairs, turned to watch and dutifully took off his T shirt. When he got back to the garage apartment Bonnie was waiting for him with a simple question, "What's all the shit?"

Creighton stared at her and finally said, "God, I hope Nick finds us here. God I hope so. Maybe he can rescue us."

Chapter Eleven

The next morning, R. Abner Dillon met Ava in the kitchen around 7:15 a.m. before Solly awoke. He had promised to come "a few days before the Deposition," to rehearse once again what Solly should say. With a knowing insouciance Dillon greeted Ava with a long kiss.

"How's Abu Ghraib evolving?" he asked smiling and apparently getting set for a second kiss.

"I think the boys are tiring of the game, and Solly spoiled things by trying to video it all."

"Jesus," Dillon said, "Solly has no concept of evidence, does he?"

"Not your sensitivity, indeed."

"A loose cannon. And that's why I'm here at this ungodly hour."

"Not so ungodly. In fact I rather enjoy the quiet solitude of it. The usual black coffee?" she asked.

He nodded and unbuttoned his grey suit coat, revealing a faded maroon vest. He often seemed to strike a pose, as if fixing himself in the scene would radiate a certain acceptance and possible command.

He knew the Dillon name commanded attention in D.C. although he often reminded outsiders that he himself did not come from the "financial side of the family." Still he took enormous pride in what he assumed his heritage ensured. He was a short man, somewhat portly and given to pale colored cufflinked shirts, often in soft shades of blue and beige. Various uncles and a great grandparent had held important positions in the U.S. treasury. Despite Covid, lineage he believed still counted for a great deal in D.C.

"Perhaps you need to rouse the great man. I have meetings today, you know." Dillon said quietly. "Besides you tell me he's not his best in the morning, isn't that so? Somewhat flaccid in the morning quite unlike normal males, or at least someone like, say, Saif, for instance."

"Why so bitchy at the start of this lovely day?"

"Bitchy? I've been called a lot of things, but bitchy wasn't one of them."

"Maybe people don't read you well."

"Maybe so, but be that as it may, we need to get Solly up to speed for next week. Not only erect but correctly erect, don't you think?"

"I'll check on him,"Ava said and exited through the swinging door.

Dillon wondered the door wound down to stillness, if had been too personal in such references to Abu Ghraib. Could it be it was not a game for Ava, but a way out of something, not a safety valve on something clearly unsustainable, but rather a novel pathway to a different life. He really wondered, if that were the case for Ava, how did he fit in? A point, he decided, worth additional exploration. After all, he could barely imagine how she found Solly even mildly interesting. No lineage. No substance, only dogged commitment. Why hadn't they introduced a dog in the cellar frolic?

There were plenty in the actual Abu Ghraib, and Muslims were terrified of them. He would have enjoying see the naked Hassans terrified of a cocker spaniel. Immediately he said to himself: "perish such thoughts . . ."

But Saif's emergence through the back kitchen door torpedoed Dillon's conscious suppression.

"Ah, Mr. Dillon, I'm sorry to interrupt your breakfast. I'm looking for a notebook I think I left here last night and some clothing."

"Part of the Abu game?"

Saif laughed, "We were interrupted—some of Professor Sears' students I think. We couldn't fully unravel patriarchy's ultimate dismal effects."

"Patriarchy's final unraveling presided over, indeed directed by, Ava Sears?" Dillon asked at the same time he conjured an image of Saif naked under a sheet.

"In late stage Capitalism, as the Quran (blessed be it) noted, women begin wearing men's trousers. Where it ends we were just exploring, when Sears' students spoiled things."

"So long as it doesn't end in violence and atrocity, I could care less where it ends up."

"Caring less is pre-eminently the American disease, isn't it? I believe somebody wrote—it's every American's dream to have enough money so as not to care—. It seems like a bad indifference to every kind of inflicted damage."

"Maybe it's too early in the day for such dark thoughts." Dillon said.

"Yes, I learned a great new American expression to dispose of dark thoughts: 'Kick the can down the road.'"

"Yes, that's true to our history. All our great compromises kicked the conflict-can down the road. But delaying needless deaths seems pretty worthy to me. How about to you?"

"Not so worthy since needed deaths demand examination, discussion, resolution. But beyond kicking the can, the Americans really learned to overlook, and deny until, and it's another great American expression, 'until the cows come home.' Inflicted suffering will never be acknowledged by colonial power, and never was."

"You and Mahmoud seemed to enjoy your collars and the cords."

"Only to learn how to pull the rope and envelope the holder."

"Is that what we were doing? I thought it was a new way to orgasm."

"It was and is. I do believe it. Violence is liberation. Liberty is detonation. Auto asphyxiation is one, clear path."

"Jesus! Undergraduate minds do run amuck."

"I'm almost twenty-three," Saif insisted.

"Well, you really ought to act your age." Dillon said. "I usually act mine."

"Except in the cellar," Saif pointed to the floor.

"Frolic will as frolic does."

"Especially as power and suffering play together."

"Sometimes you seem to forget that I came here in an effort to keep you and Mahmoud out of jail."

"We're not in jail. We had nothing to do with the incident."

"Surely you're not so dumb, so naïve, to think you can't be linked to atrocity—just by who you are, what you believe, where you choose to live, by so willingly pressing your noses to the floor five times a day."

"About the life of Muslims here, you can say nothing. I know you might worry about your phrase, 'where you choose to live' Legitimate worry."

"True enough. We're knotted together in several ways, aren't we? Some of them quite relieving and enjoyable."

"They feed your needs and ours, as legitimate threats."

"What are you threatening?"

"Open discussion of our games in the cellar."

"You're more than a little viper, aren't you? A real shit."

"Survival often requires drilling through real shit."

"And what does your blessed Quran (oh, peace be upon it) say about such things?"

"The Prophet—peace be upon him—" Saif corrected, "says suffering is always an aspect of survival. Dying and thriving."

"How boring. I'll caution Solly to steer clear of theology in the deposition."

"Steer clear of Allah."

"Oh, absolutely, he seems a rather vindicative fellow, albehim a juicy one on occasion." Dillon patted Saif on his shoulder and let his palm linger there.

They both turned, hearing Creighton coming down the stairs.

"Coffee," Creighton moaned, "coffee. Soon. Now. Jesus, the dreams I'm having."

Dillon looked carefully at Creighton and finally said, "I'm not the morning help, and at my hourly rate, it's going to be costly. To say nothing of ending up indicting this lovely lad." Dillon put his palm back on Saif's shoulder.

Saif winced and said, "One of Professor Sears' students,"

"A colleague of Prof. Sears," Creighton corrected him. "Not a close colleague, purely professional fellow researcher on American Foreign Policy. And now desperate for some coffee."

With some incredulity Dillon said, "You're staying above the garage?"

"I suppose so," Creighton answered moving toward the stove.

"It's in a hot pot to the left of the back burner," Saif said with assured familiarity.

Creighton took a small brown cup out of the drying rack and filled it with coffee. "Just black," he assured anyone listening.

"I'm Abner Dillion, Ava Sears' attorney. I don't live here and neither does he," Dillon pointed to Saif. "He's just the phone boy—are you familiar with the term? In India it's just a likely lad, undoubtedly from a lower caste, who's employed to answer the phone, take a message, transcribe it and bringing it to you while you take your Lariam."

"Lariam?" Saif asked.

"A drug to keep you safe from malaria, but probably only causing heavy dreams."

"Perhaps I was slipped some last night. Jesus, the dreams I had last night. I imagined I'd killed my two-year old daughter, Jenna."

"Did you?" Saif asked.

"You don't have to answer that, and as an officer of the court I have to inform you that I must report any discussion of what clearly is a crime." Dillon said.

"Jesus! It was just a dream," Creighton said. "I'm Creighton. I'm a member of Prof. Sears' strategy seminar. I'm here, just staying a night for. . . . for complicated reasons. Nothing serious."

"Did you hurt her?" Saif asked.

"Of course I didn't. She's my only child, the only one."

"Of course he didn't. Otherwise I'd have to tell the court. Don't keep asking." Dillon said.

After a tick or two of silence, Saif said, "Sorry."

A few more seconds of silence. "Look, anybody who's tried to deal with a two year old knows murder is always an attractive option," Creighton smiled. "I know that. Doubtless Attorney Dillon knows that, and in your case," he nodded toward Saif, "I'm certain you'll get your chance to know it too."

"Americans like to kill." Saif said.

"Jesus!" Creighton said, "I only came down for a little coffee."

"I believe young Saif believes that. And doubtless has had chances to see it verified. But that doesn't make it true." Dillon said.

"Americans are good at getting others to do it for them." Saif continued. "In my country they trained a whole army to do it for them, trained them well, gave them every instrument they need to carry it out."

"Seems the seminar has come home with Solly, and that's lamentable." Dillon said. "You live here too long, Saif, and you'll pick up too much of the lingo, too much of the university game."

"You live here too?" Creighton asked.

"There," Saif pointed through the kitchen window to the carriage house. "Ever since Covid closed the dorms."

"So, Ava and Solly turn out to be generous souls when they're not training Egyptian soldiers to kill for them, is that it? Generous enough to move you into their carriage house? I just want to get it straight what you believe. The Americans are killers who train others to kill for them, but occasionally offer their homes for free to refugees? Is that it?" Dillon asked.

"Americans really like killing, look at their movies and their T.V. shows. That's clear enough. Killing satisfies them as a way of settling everything. You know that. But there's enough residue of Biblical injunction to make them seem kind. Guilty and kind. But thoughtlessly butchering."

"Seems like Solly might need to get a new phone boy," Creighton said, guardedly chuckling.

"Or at least a more grateful one. You know the reason I'm here it this kitchen this morning is to help Solly keep young Saif here out of the investigation of the recent 'incident' a little pro bono gesture to those we allegedly keep killing." Dillon said. "And here's the gratitude I get for this help."

"We get to re-enact the fun side of your torture at Abu Ghraib. Maybe we should invite Mr. Creighton into that?" Saif said slowly and smiling.

Dillon thought, the kid is a cunning manipulator and should be paid attention to beyond his splendid bodily ministrations. Tuck that information in the back of your mind, Abner, Dillon concluded, while speaking: "I doubt colleague Creighton has the appetite or moral depravity to be a full participant. Don't you agree?"

"You're asking me?" Creighton said. "Lately I've been game for anything, including hurting my only child."

"All you have to do is link that atrocity with some personal need, say, for example, personal freedom, and all is forgiven in this land of, and for, the people." Saif said.

"Such patriotism," Dillon noted, "earns its own rewards—say, all expenses for a trip to Niagara Falls, U.S. side only."

"I actually took the misty boat to the other side and I still have that nifty blue transparent poncho they give you to keep you dry. It was truly impressive. Nature redeems America!" Saif said.

Creighton added, "Seems I don't get the subtext here."

"It's true, the expansive American landscape hides a whole lot of dirty dealing. What's excessive profit compared to Niagara Falls?" Dillon said. "How do the Falls overflow a dozen ejaculations? Can there really be a comparison?"

"It would take meticulous measurements," Creighton said, chuckling.

Ava pushed on the swinging door, opening it about six inches. "Solly's waiting for you in the living room—sorry to break up this conversation."

"We'd run out of righteous gas, hadn't we anyway?" Dillon said as he moved through the door. "I can help Solly get through the mess."

2.

There was almost thirty seconds of silence as Creighton and Saif looked at each other.

At length Creighton said, "You seem disappointed in America."

For an answer Saif said, "How did you hurt your daughter?"

With instant and surprising matter-of-factness Creighton replied, "I drowned her in a bathtub with her friend, Sybil."

"Both girls?"

"Yes," Creighton answered, "both girls at once. Sybil's mother, Bonnie, helped me. She's upstairs now."

"Americans are gifted killers. Automatic and unfeeling." Saif said with equal matter-of-factness.

"Oh, don't imagine that. I hate myself every day for what we did."

"But only after the fact." Saif pressed on. "Even now, you seem easy with it. Isn't that so?"

"It's done. I can't change that. But I wish I could. How I wish that."

Saif smiled, "No crying over spilt milk—is that it?"

"You can't make an omelet without breaking some eggs . . ." Creighton added. "I can easily out adage you with American sayings."

Saif came very close to Creighton, leaned into his face and said quietly, "Allah sees the cracked egg of your heart and heals it."

"I don't believe that," Creighton said.

"It doesn't matter what you believe. It is so."

"And will Allah give me back my Jenna?"

"Never. But you will find her in some other form."

"A nice idea, but a stupid hope."

"It is so."

Creighton pondered that assertion but finally said, "I just came down to get some coffee."

"And I told you where it was," Saif answered. "Tonight come down to our Abu Ghraib game. You'll learn even more, and we'll all welcome you. Bring Bonnie with you."

Chapter Twelve

Solly and Ava usually began preparing for what they thought of as "full scale re-creation" of Abu Ghraib by watching thirty-five minutes of home videos made in the prison at the time. Where and how these came to be wasn't clear; what was clear is that they had the commanding aura of authenticity. Their amateur camera angles, their occasional blurriness, their stale, gritty, near black and white pallor all signaled first-time novice production. As documentary they were embarrassing; as art they were imbecilic; as stimulant they were intoxicating. Watching them Solly often proclaimed brought back sweet memories of his golden boot-camp days, watching in the barrack's attic bootlegged copies of pornography projected on a sagging white sheet screen. It seemed the actors- in both productions displayed similar uneasiness about what they were doing—a kind of constant desperate looking-over-their-shoulders for would-be moral, hostile enforcers. But enforcing what? For American porn, perhaps inadequate makeup? Obese bodies? Insufficiently convincing blood—residue of ketchup, water, and wholesale canola oil? For happenstance Iraqi prison documentaries, the screaming was disturbingly on target, the mutilations hardly staged, the writhing bodies naked and nipped by howling dogs fiercely suggestive and for Ava and Solly enthralling. Witnessing such staged, restless nakedness was captivating, then arousing.

And once arousing soon pressed into necessary ritual, so that nothing could sexually happen between them without this essential video foreplay. "Like stretching before yoga," Ava acknowledged in daylight.

The video was only amuse buse to the in-person re-enactments that Saif had suggested they witness to understand the thinking of truly exploited peoples. Moreover, by putting on and throwing off the collars, the leashes, the whips, the insisted-on canine grapplings, exploiters and exploiters could fully embrace, become one in glorious sexual congress so that mixing of fluids would accelerate spiritual fusion and true grasp of otherness. Magically satiated peace could supplant negotiated, and unfulfilling peace among hostile parties. Magically satiated peace—MSP the greatest possible acronym in the new world order so dreamed of by deluded western thinkers who could only imagine such achievement via rational discourse, and who therefore were doomed to yearn and yearn and never learn and learn—what their loins could show them in a flash of supreme excitement. Saif's and Mahmoud's rhetoric issued persuasiveness just as their nakedness enticed their leering, elder audience.

They usually began the general striptease by taking opposite ends of the cellar under dimmable mini floodlights mounted in the white stucco ceiling. And from those opposing points began a back-and-forth political dialogue. And tonight was no exception. Mahmoud as always spoke first as he began unbuttoning his shirt, a vibrantly blue poplin collarless garment over a jet black athletic sleeveless T shirt.

"America begins with the usurpation of native peoples—the slaughter of innocent Indians whose technology could not match white weaponry. And whose values could not grasp the idea of victory by medicinal infection. What a beginning for your America!"

From the other end of the cellar came Saif's echo: "What a beginning for your America! Slaughter of innocents via infection, via virus, via a soulless assertion that their very inhabitance of land meant they had to die. What a beginning for your America! Otherness meant death. OMD the new acronym of your very existence." Saif had taken off his khaki trousers and displayed blue spandex underwear.

"Take it off, all of it!" shouted Ava.

"And get down on all fours, you cur!" added Solly. "Get ready for your collar."

Mahmoud said, "You cannot treat humans like dogs. Dogs deserve only death."

"So die!" Ava screamed.

"Love," Solly said, "You're getting ahead of the game. Premature ejaculation spoils everything."

Creighton and Bonnie had come down the stairs to watch, and suddenly Creighton grew energized by what he witnessed. Mahmoud was entirely naked, but Saif seemed bashful about removing his trunks. Solly had shed his shirt and his Landsend grey T shirt. And all seemed to acknowledge that Ava, under her floral orange bathrobe, had already disrobed.

Creighton jumped down to the cellar floor with boundless enthusiasm and shouted, "Yes premature ejaculation spoils everything, leads back to self-restraint, doesn't it?"

"But you Americans have none, do you? You measure your life by the distractions you accumulate, weighing worth by things and despairing of finding any peace. You're constant in your worship of disruption.," Mahmoud proclaimed, turning to display very hairy buttocks.

"Yes! Disruption! Naked disruption!" shouted Saif, kicking away his trunks, and furiously unbuttoning his shirt. "Open your robe, Mrs. Sears!"

The formality of the term lent a sudden, stumbling block to the growing arousal, as if the group had heard and obeyed some distant chastisement from a loudspeaker hidden in their consciousness. Could it be that duly married adults could enter this game? Could a Mrs. become somehow free enough to disrobe entirely? Wouldn't the use of "Mrs." toss everything retrograde, unspontaneous, and anon, polluted. Indeed, hadn't it already done that? Fortunately, there was a double closure of any threatened taming down of the coming orgy.

Simultaneously Ava cast aside her floral orange robe, knotting into a weird genital-protecting wad, and then just dropping it to the linoleum, where it seemed to caress the cracked and flaking green residue swirl of the aged tile. And at the same time, Bonnie joined Creighton and began unbuttoning her blouse and tugging down her brown tweed skirt.

"Yes!" Saif shouted, "anything premature is just proper preparation, like soaking the proffered blankets with cholera or maybe bubonic plague and presenting them to the naked and hapless recipients."

"Let's remember who the recipients were and are here," Solly asserted. "Kneel down and take your collars."

As if to underscore and carry out Solly's orders, Bonnie confronted Mahmoud and suddenly took hold of his scrotum, yanking him toward her. "On your knees! Native riff-raft."

"There's a woman worthy to be President!" Solly laughed shouting.

Seizing on what he thought the game culminated in, Mahmoud hauled Bonnie to him, clamping her body and locking tight her arms with his surrounding grip so that she couldn't pull him anywhere and with an intensity that if she tried closing her hand as defense he would crush the life out of her, and then quickly he bent them both to the floor and began mock humping her while nuzzling off her half-undone bra.

Creighton in a frenzy rushed over and yanked on Mahmoud's hair trying to free Bonnie.

Saif rushed to the enmeshed twosome and screamed. "Release her my brother. We've not run through their 'Manifest Destiny' phase, their pillaging of Spanish possessions to the South and beyond the great ocean to our Filipino brothers, all in the squirrel-like imitation of British imperial dreams. Their sick partitioning of the world and their stupid ravaging, all before we take our glorious revenge. And relieve ourselves in them."

"Revenge?" Creighton asked. "I thought this was a consensual orgy."

"Oh, it is," Solly answered, "the brothers get carried away, so we leash them and call them back, don't we Ava darling?"

"Oh, I suppose that is the formula in the past at least. I never like calling Saif back," she smiled.

Mahmoud stood back up and Bonnie, laughing, got to her feet.

"In our embarrassing haste we omitted a fundamental step, fundamental saturation before ecstasy." Solly said.

"Yes," Saif acknowledged, "we forgot the Hookahs, the basic bong effect," he laughed.

"And we have truly excellent hash, as our contribution." Creighton added.

Solly opened the standing armoire near the entrance to the furnace area and took out two large hookah pipes already filled with clouded water. Creighton ran back upstairs to get his hash.

Bonnie spoke quietly to Mahmoud, "Sorry, I didn't understand the rules. I still don't, I'm afraid, but I'll wait to be led."

"We change the rules," Mahmoud answered, "depending on a number of things."

"Things?" Bonnie said.

"Lots of things—whips, chains, ropes—But always in the context of explaining why history moves so directly when the U.S. is involved. From land grab to attempted heart grab to eventual market grab with a trailing culture grab, soon enough, distraction grab so that no one quite perceives what has occurred. We include when it seems most proper certain 'safe words,' to limit the action. At all times we know what we're doing."

"Or we think we do," Ava added.

The arranging of two hookah pipes, the sloshing of fresh water filling them, took a while and the group seemed less satisfied with their nakedness. The room felt cold.

"Dillon always upped the heat before," Ava said. "It was his contribution."

"A small, disappointing offering," Solly said, drawing the first long inhalation from his lavender colored pipe. The Hassan boys always opted first for the green pipe. They sat cross-legged on the linoleum and took incremental puffs in contrast to Solly's long, sustained sucking.

Bonnie and Ava giggled at their turn, but soon enough the room for them seemed to swell and shrink in a lovely ingratiating way.

"Best hash ever," Creighton sighed slumping into an orange floor pillow."

"Time for discipline and payback," Solly said noisily.

"No, resting always wins," Saif said, "on Sunday afternoons we always sit in wicker chairs, and survey the hills from our bamboo porches and take our Lariam, don't we? Or did I mix up empires?"

"Yes, you fool," Mahmoud chastised his brother. "We only swill down burgers and dream of our precious containment policy and wallow in our atomic weaponry. No need for Lariam now, we have, for certain, a vaccine!"

"Yes, and endless plans to impose blessed democracy on hapless victims of our atrocities."

"Who gives a shit about politics? Let's ease further toward true understanding," Ava said, taking soft hold of Saif's considerable genitals.

"Is it impolitic to ask now whether we're all vaccinated?" Creighton asked.

"Too late," Ava answered, stroking Saif toward full arousal.

'It's not too late to decry American faith in rat psychology,' Mahmoud said, pushing away the proffered pipe. "Your belief that powerful threats maintain harmony in the world, the deepest cynicism that you hold the keys of dominance alone among nations."

"I'm hooking you up, leashing you, boy, to keep that crap talk where it belongs, in caves with your brothers." Solly said, snaping the leash chain on to Mahmoud's fur-lined collar.

"It's time we put these boys under sheets," Solly said, dropping his leash. He went back to the armoire and took out three neatly folded white sheets. "These lend authenticity to our efforts. Who gets the one with the head hole tonight?"

"Ah," Saif said, "who gets to be the field hand or house boy. The role Dillon always, always, rejected."

"Who's Dillon?" Bonnie asked.

"No matter, just another intruder from the government," Solly answered. "He's not playing tonight."

"I miss Dillon," Ava added. "He lent order, discipline, structure, but on the other hand he was the absolute enemy of spontaneity."

"Fuck spontaneity." Someone said.

"On the contrary," Solly said, tossing a sheet over Mahmoud. "We need to shroud these lads from themselves, else they'll never really enter the game."

"Oh, I will." Saif insisted.

"Yes, he will," Ava said. "I've seen it before, felt it before, experienced it before, and I so want to feel it again."

Solly spread the second sheet over Mahmoud, letting his head emerge from the whiteness. "Now we're set to begin the recreation. Maybe tonight we can forfeit the brutality and stress innate kindness. What, after all, we deeply believe about our natural American desires."

"Yes, our natural kindness and concerns for others," Ava said softly and laughing as she squatted on all fours and ducked under Saif's sheet.

"Ohh, ooohh, such a kind lady," Saif gradually said.

"Brother! Where's your concern for Manifest Destiny now, eh? What's next? The Christian message? Can you so shallowly spurt away Filipino independence?"

"Spurt away," Solly shouted, "these trash natives are slaves to their loins."

And he slumped down, semi-squatting on the linoleum and then toppling over in a haze of sudden appreciation for the swirling green-ness beneath him and the swirling beige walls and Ava's soft wet moaning as Saif moved from receptor to aggressor. Solly lay back and imagined himself above the tableau and watching Dillon cracking a whip to remove the sheets so that all were revealed in oily beads of desire and disappointment while Mahmoud droned on his itemization of American incursions and punishments toward the freedoms of the exploited.

"From the sabotage of Mossadegh to the unbelievable slicing of Gaddafi, you Americans have played lethal games in our glorious culture trying to infest our minds with your rancid consumerism, and your cavalier dismissal of all butchery. And while fomenting discord and slaughter in other lands, in your own you smash family tradition, institutionalize separateness and watch with celebration the breakdown of all norms by which any community thrives. The worship of market capitalism leads directly to the incineration of Hiroshima."

"Jesus!" Solly said, "find some distraction. Your recitations are tiring."

"Yes," Ava shouted, "take up with somebody, for God's sake."

Mahmoud stood up and slowly swiveling observing the coupling going on said loudly "Allah cannot be mocked with such filth."

Bonnie digging fingers into Mahmoud's calfs said almost plaintively. "I'm here. I want the big Arab. Solly, make him obey!"

Dutifully Solly yanked on the clothesline attached to Mahmoud's collar, which only made Mahmoud yank the line out of Solly's seared hands. He then pulled Bonnie up to him by her hair. "Enter my harem," Mahmoud laughed nervously, and encircled her with the line.

"Jesus," Creighton sighed, collapsing on another soft purple pillow on the floor. "This the best hash ever," he said, taking another long toke from the hookah. "You got that right about distractions, brother. You got that so right. But you didn't say how to get free of them. So they dance around you throttling your sense of self and leeringly pulling you into a pit with no bottom, no sidewalls either. Vapor of nothingness yet full of slashing knives inflicting tiny cuts for each longing of mutuality or connection, till you can't move, can't breathe, can't even sigh. And then you hear the lustrous voice of consolation ordering you to take action, the soul action to end the fluid of distraction—to commit the ultimate and perfect atrocity, the murder of children, your own children."

That enunciation seemed to stun the lust-loosed, squirrel it back into a cage of some kind, make it seem untoward, unworthy—a distraction from distractedness.

"What's your point?" Solly asked, apparently perplexed. If there are steps we need to take, tell us."

As if answer to that question there was thunderous knocking on the front door, and then a slamming of that barrier and clomping through the hall to the dining room and suddenly a dark, immense figure looming at the top of cellar stairs.

"Good God!" Bonnie wailed, "it's Nick. He's found us!"

2.

"Intruder! Come join us. Surely you are our deliverance from the vile ruminations of that low rent fossil." Solly pointed toward Creighton.

Nick lurching down the steps so that his inertia sent him making frenzied dance moves to avoid toppling over, still had ample breath to shout, "You fucking, lying bitch where are you storing my Sybil? Where, Bonnie? Where? You'll tell me, won't you!" He grabbed Bonnie by her left shoulder and spun her to the ground, simultaneously thrusting the side of his right palm into Mahmoud's neck.

"Wait! Wait!" Solly shouted, "that sort of violence is not part of this game. You need to learn the parameters. You must observe the boundaries!"

"Boundaries! Fuck your boundaries! You'll tell me where you're hiding Sybil, or I'll kill your fucking boyfriend."

"Who's Sybil?" Ava asked.

"Shut the fuck up." Nick answered.

Groggily Mahmoud tried to stand up, only eliciting another vicious chop from Nick. Mahmoud crumpled to the floor again, and apparently to underscore his rage, Nick kicked Mahmoud in the stomach, making a sloppy thudding sound. Mahmoud gasped and yelped.

Creighton backed away and thought about bolting up the stairs but reconsidered believing Nick's step might be to kick Bonnie. There was a brief tableau with figures apparently frozen in place, the question of Sybil lingering in the grey, sweet air.

Solly said, "Please take a toke. It will make everything fall into place. No need to escalate an already fraught situation. No need."

"Fraught? What the fuck is 'fraught'?"

"Believe me, if you don't understand 'fraught' there's no hope for the situation." Solly said, smiling.

Nick turned and launched a streaking right cross punch that sent Solly's two upper front teeth skittering across the linoleum. Saif in a low crouch rushed to his brother's side. "You've hurt him bad." Saif said, taking off his sheet and putting it over Mahmoud.

Solly toppled and after a long moment of shock started crawling after his teeth. He found one tooth against the first step of the stairs. Solly leaned the side of his head on the step and tried to insert the tooth back into its hole, but the rushing blood suddenly nauseated him, and he coughed and vomited while still prone on the linoleum.

"Jesus," Ava said softly watching Solly's collapse.

"Where's Sybil? If I don't get an answer, I'm gonna kill all of ya." Nick yelled.

That threat seemed to energize Creighton who felt himself tighten toward combat or perhaps certain death—Yes, that was the beckoning he suddenly felt, indeed worshipped. He could save Jenna from Nick and at the same time obliterate the punishment he so deserved for drowning her. Suddenly there was remotely stirring joy, such as he had never encountered before, a surge of pleasurable emptying as if unendurable poundage had been lifted away and he ran straight at Nick, as if rushing deliriously straight into a speeding diesel train engine, one that guaranteed to splatter him into a billion-minute shards. "Awwggah!" he howled throwing himself at Nick who sidestepped and kneed Creighton in the face and neck crunching Creighton's larynx.

Ava stood over Solly's whimpering body at the bottom of the stairs and said with icy, near elegant articulation, "Saif, help your brother get back to the carriage house and Nick, if that is your name, take Creighton over there too. I'd rather he die out of my house. I'm sure you understand. Solly, get yourself up and go to the downstairs bathroom. Clean yourself up. We'll put the teeth in later, much later. Too many things to solve now. Bonnie, come with me. It's time to call Dillon."

Chapter Thirteen

Almost two hours elapsed before Dillon arrived. He carefully examined the cellar, came back upstairs, and talked quietly with Ava and a sobbing Solly. "Don't fret about the hearing. You can get that delayed. Solly, the story is you tripped going downstairs and there may be a mild concussion, don't you think? I think so, and we'll get your doctor to examine you later tomorrow, won't we? You heard some mayhem downstairs and clearly there was a threatening tone toward your wife. You were worried she was in danger, and that led to extra hustle and the fall. Do you understand, Solly? Just stick to that story. Your worry. Your haste, and your fall. It's a simple story and very believable. Ava, your story is more elaborate, and a lot will depend on how convincing you are. I'm sure you understand that."

"I do," Ava said.

"It's not a marriage story," Dillon laughed. "It's just designed, if you accomplish it fully, to get rid of the evidence, all of it." Dillon got up from the couch in the living room and moved to the sliding glass doors to the sunroom/porch, something he had told them to install last spring. Dillon admired the precision of the doors and golden yellow color

Ava had chosen for the one side wall and the ceiling. Was it moonlight reflected off those surfaces, Dillon wondered, or just residual light from the living room? Dillon turned back, "Listen carefully, Ava. And I know you can, but this is a bit tricky, requires a certain focus and commitment on your part. And I know you can handle it. Over time the Hassan boys have begun to confide in you—nothing like a full confession, but some allusions to *The Incident*, that led you to believe they had more of a hand in that calamity than they had previously indicated. They seemed troubled by *The Incident*, regretful, maybe even guilty, but not confessional, although it might be Saif was far more contrite than his brother. Couldn't that be so? It might be expected. Not specific evidence but something bothering both of them. Got it? You were concerned for them, even motherly." Dillon smiled. "Yes motherly. Definitely concerned and when you suggested they should turn to the authorities, they reacted strangely, even hostilely, as if they regretted mentioning anything to you. They became more agitated as Mahmoud worried out loud that you might take matters into your own hands. That's what Solly heard. That's what alarmed Solly. Anyone might have felt the same, Isn't that so? "

"They'll deny it," Ava said.

"Of course, they would, if given the chance. That's why the next step is so crucial. You do it well, and they won't get a chance to deny anything. So, the next step is essential. You'll need to rehearse it carefully. You'll call 911 in a few moments and alert them that you've been threatened by your very tenants, by the very students you've housed for free because of Covid and the closed dorms, by the very souls you've taken under your wing, by the fellows you've tried to help. They've mentioned some connection with *The Incident* and then have made you feel afraid. You know they have weapons in the carriage house. You've seen them. Someone needs to contain them. You're frightened of them. Do you understand? You need to make the call. They're at the carriage house. You don't know what they might do. You need to convey danger, immediate danger."

"Hysterical?" Ava asked.

"You're never hysterical. You're a member of the court. Hysterics are forbidden, aren't they?" Dillon said smiling. "Can you make the call now? Imminent danger. Swat team possibility etc. etc. Then when they get here, a chance misfire and who knows what might happen? Who knows who might be killed? Link to *The Incident* somehow. Make the call, Ava. Make the call, Ava. There was an altercation in your cellar. An altercation. Your guest was hurt, left unconscious and bleeding on your cellar floor. You were threatened. They retreated to the carriage house. They're there now, with weapons, and God knows what else. You've opened your home to danger, to demons. Make the call, Ava. Be convincing. Inertia will do the rest."

manuscript ends here . . .

Part V

Aftermath and Unsturdy Effacement

[your eye, my thumb]*
*no further manuscript discovered. . . .

A Somewhat Appreciative Afterword
by C. Livingston Wells

The manuscript Thomas Ausa left behind illustrated his mediocrity in two separate fields—history and fiction. He imagined the one would illuminate the other, but that didn't happen. His weird, alleged magnum opus, titled, "American Foreign Policy—A Novel," floundered between those disciplines and eventually expired waiting for a rescue tide that never came. He may well have thought that since an enormous pitching of the sea had tossed the text onto dry beach land, that an equal wave surely would carry it back to hallowed, aspired, ocean depths. One more disappointment. The little literary leaving baked in the Florida sunlight, turned sour in the moonlight, and grew putrid in its dismissal.

But perhaps I have been too dismissive. When I was Deputy Chief of Mission in too many countries to list, that was often the charge—I was too hasty, too abrasive, but I flatter myself that I did learn the diplomatic arts; studying the Thais was more than helpful. More than any other people they know how to differ without irritating, know how to disagree without rancor, know how to move people off hardened positions to see the wisdom the Thais espouse. It's miraculous, but I digress.

To begin at the beginning. One has to grapple with an admittedly truncated book entitled "American Foreign Policy, A Novel," that has nothing to do with American Foreign Policy. So I remarked to Thomas that simply adding "A Novel" to the title was not adequate clue to any reader that the ensuing voyage would be difficult to swallow, so to speak, and Thomas, characteristically did not catch my joke.

It was one third finished and that ought to be acknowledged in his defense. He was clear enough in explaining his technique: first a presentation of what he considered the basic themes of American international relations, presented in segmented form, a chapter for each, followed by what he imagined were compelling short narratives illustrating fictionally his perceptions of American diplomacy across time. It turned out he didn't get much beyond labelling the themes, merely titling them at the start of each Part. No elaboration, no orderly presentation of the argument with evidence for each Part. Nothing beyond the title and even that marking reduced to a minimum of text. He assured me there were pages and pages of exposition illuminating the themes. No one could be disappointed at their immediate absence; reams awaited the diligent devotee who had a knowledge of Ausa's work ethic. They were, he assured me and several others in a very safe, fire-proof place and only needed some "polishing" before he inserted them after the epigraph of each chapter. Inquiries about their whereabouts only elicited mocking laughter and a modest sermon on faith in his truthfulness. I never believed him. In fact, he was inherently lazy, a born conceptualizer and an utterly unfocused, uncommitted realizer. (Is that a word?). So, the actual legacy is the narrative, fictional part of the manuscript—just the story, so to speak and the reader is left to ponder how the "thematic" epigraph relates to the rich panoply of American diplomatic history.

Ausa did believe, as do I, that stories are the essence of educational transfer, not logical, evidence backed, argument. I'm pretty certain by the time he had a written a third of the fictional narrative he had no juice left for presentation of the history of his analysis of American foreign relations. In fact, analysis was not his forte. He was much better at suggesting historical resonances in the pornography he relished creating. As for example in the bizarre re-enactments Ava and Solly Sears undertake with the Hassan boys of Abu Ghraib's excesses. He of course put into Saif's naïve mouth sentiments he liked to say he himself believed. Or at least he was occasionally fond of saying: "Saif speaks for me." He often claimed "resonances" could do what he called the heavy lifting of grasping policy. I thought that was specious. It was specious, and I pointed out his references to Nick as somehow related to force preponderance simply didn't work. His rejoinder was inevitable: "Liv, all you're saying is that for you resonances don't work." He spent a whole afternoon intoning to me that Nick's instant fury and strength corresponded perfectly to America's atomic excesses, but what a futile effort on his part, almost a sickness.

In fact his own health issues undoubtedly dictated incising his ambitions for the work. Were those health issues real? A question that perhaps deserves a modest sidebar. Admittedly there were creditable markers. He did have a mild heart attack in 2001. Stents (the Italian doctors called them "stints") were inserted and a standard statin dosage begun which would continue for the next twenty years, something like 50 milligrams twice a day. And in 2006, while he was still teaching there was an episode of what most physicians came to label as "Guillain Barre" syndrome, weakening or removing the sheaths around the nerves in his feet and shins, so that he had balance problems and some difficulty walking. But he only flirted occasionally with using a cane, but toward the end he did hump over a bit in walking and used railings, chair edges, door handles with excessive dependency. Don't we all after a certain age, until we grip the pewter handle of our blasted dreams as we enter our heavenly peace?

I did have the always regretted proclivity of engaging him on the meaning of his terse epigraphs, and if the mood hit him, he would lay out the substance of his argument concerning each assertion. Sometimes he made persuasive sense, but more often than not he retreated to the messy windbag posture of his teaching, confident that his 18 to 22 yr. old audience would be dazzled by his allusions and knowing references to utterly invented facts.

I inquired for example about his bifurcation in the very first epigram "The Open Door and the Closed Heart" and he quickly brought up something he called 'The Wisconsin School' apparently closet Marxists who seemed to think Secretary John Hay's enunciation of the Open Door in 1898 explained the fundamental driving force of American foreign policy—the insistence on the free trade among nations, a gloriously open competition that would always ensure American domination. The arch enemy therefore was the Closed Door, sealing off of the American Market—forcing that Door Open required whatever it would take, from missionary entreaty, to military intervention. Keeping the Door Open provided for these fellows the motivation and rationale for U.S. foreign policy. Simultaneously and as a necessary tandem, that policy required a closed heart to the effects of opening that Door, whether it be conversion to Christianity, or simple torture and slaughter or removal of resistant peoples, initially natives—Indians, later imported black slaves, later still Spaniards, or Frenchmen, or British, immigrant hordes, anyone who attempted to keep The Open Door even partially closed. So, image became a kind of prism to breakdown the infinite data of diplomacy into economically driven strands—the agricultural market, the iron steel market, the manufactured goods market, etc. etc. All were seen as robotic soldiers shoving their interests into the hopper of policy.

On the individual level Creighton understood, indeed internalized, the process and came to believe only a private horrendous act could liberate him, re-integrate him in some higher than market realm. A realm he didn't believe in, although he knew his closed heart kept him from knowing. His was an agony/ tension that required an obliterating resolution. And he found at least two: Jenna and Sybil both drowned perhaps accidentally through a haze of drugs, alcohol, and simple lust for autonomy. Reduction of foreign policy to mathematical data was enticing but ultimately self- defeating. After calculations poor Creighton was still there wondering why things actually occurred. Eventually Creighton believed he lived only for distractions against his supremely leftover feelings and to be free of distractions he needed only to commit one monstrous atrocious act. Atrocity was liberation and he rushed toward it with unthinking glee.

Then in a dizzying shift, toward the end, Ausa was more or less certain that all explanation for anything, certainly anything so schematic as foreign policy, could be best explained by linguistic inquiry. Dissecting the rhetoric of policy makers could yield the best rationale for why the policy was accepted, since words best explained it to decision makers. Ausa apparently thought certain frames of language inevitably led to certain policy decisions irrespective of either the market drives, or the ideological prompts, or the economic imperatives, or the media hype. Every action he insisted resided in its linguistic structure, or in the ways decision makers expressed their wishes. I didn't quite follow it, and in truth even Ausa didn't quite follow it, I do believe.

If Open Door/Closed Heart didn't explain policy ultimately or even legitimately, it certainly did shed great light on certain frames of expression like "Manifest Destiny" or "Containment" or "Preserving the Free World," or "Making the World Safe for Democracy," or more recently "Building New Nations," or "Regime Change." Keeping the Door Open unlocked such focuses, didn't it? Did it explain the closed heart decision Creighton and Bonnie so casually make concerning their progeny?

But such a vision ultimately reduced fellows like me to base economic motives and we didn't cotton to it. And that was for me the great puzzle of Ausa's approach. He had such particular and peculiar reverence for fellows like me, old line Foreign Service Officers with impeccable East Coast credentials, such noble family stock. He listened to us, fawned around us like the silly ferret he was gathering our nuggets of inherited lingo and panache and even believing our mottos and nostrums about duty, country, and whatever else crap MacArthur liked to invoke as he wept over his defeats and embarrassments and chanted on Annapolis's plains, "duty, honor, country."

So Ausa tossed up additional frames. The frame of "Containment" surely explained the post atomic world of the 20th century, especially with its two bastard offspring—"Force preponderance" and "Asymmetrical Warfare." But were we really to believe that the Hassan boys were engaging in some kind of quasi terrorist asymmetrical warfare by re-staging luridly the excesses of Abu Ghraib? Was blue spandex really the vehicle of asymmetry? Of course, it wasn't, he insisted, but the erotic did have a role in proper instruction to get at the truth, even Socrates admitted as much, Thomas declared, as if that invocation of Greek authority settled the argument. More importantly, he went on, asymmetry had only begun to recognize the tyranny of technology in its evolution. What evolution I asked, but he brushed aside that objection and continued with a hymn to the "governing structures" of technology in policy-makers' decisions.

He announced the technological innovation of the helicopter dictated General Westmoreland's strategic obsession with "search and destroy" in America's tragic sojourn into the war in Vietnam. Moreover, the whole of American participation could be best explained by the development of the containerized shipping industry which made America's interference possible. Finally, the success of America's technology in the creation of that apex of human disfigurement, atomic bombs on Hiroshima and Nagasaki, underscored the theme/frame of rat psychology which drove America's policy from the incursion against native peoples in the seventeenth century to the present exploration of Mars. Ah, breathtaking I could only applaud such sentiments, but naturally Thomas did not grasp my joke. How his undergraduates must have lapped up such sweeping indictments!

Within the novel I did like, and I did get the mayhem of the Hassans and Nick's truculence, and Creighton's maundering madness and Ava's sharp-eyed focus on her own pleasure all blended toward some sort of summation of Mutual Assured Destruction of every American dream of policy's ultimate aim in the post atomic, post atrocity world. The themes/frames might explain the history of American Foreign Policy but they don't explain American foreign policy. Or so I told him continually, but he really didn't listen.

Some readers have asked me to comment on the validity of the themes/frames of his view of American foreign policy, and I am delighted to do so. I did admire talking with Thomas Ausa. I did not always follow his "framing" of policy. And, quite frankly, I've not regretted dismissing most of his meandering structures. His whole notion of theme-ing/framing he insisted came from his long study of the so called "content analysis" wing of artificial intelligence investigation. He found what he deeply believed was the basic structure of language grasp, the setting up of "frames" or "themes" of language use that he argued determined understanding of words used in communication. Somehow, he felt that such frames determined where policy was headed, determined how it was thought about, and braced how it was implemented. Thus he believed if he could identify the themes/frames of discourse, that policy makers unconsciously develop within particular cultures, he could predict what policies would come to pass.

If the Open Door and the Closed Heart were not just after the fact labels but rather were the very way reality was grasped by policy makers then their next moves or any moves could be discerned and compensated for. Similarly, if "containment" was not just a policy but rather theme/frame of perceived reality—and Ausa passionately believed containment rat psychology—the notion that force worked always to change behavior, that punishment always altered behavior to match the policy maker's intention, then Containment or what Ausa insisted was better termed, "encircling force" explained how things would go in American diplomacy. It was tiresome then, and now, listening to him pontificate of such matters. And he couldn't be joshed out of it.

So, I pushed him on what the conclusion of the novel really was going to be.

He seemed delighted to be asked and quickly proffered the following: 1) Nick and the Hassans and Creighton, who really suffered some brain damage and excessive bleeding retreated to the carriage house, and maybe Bonnie—Thomas had not decided on that. They holed up there and waited to see Dillon's next move, but he had already called the police and other security forces, had already been howling "terrorists" etc. So soon enough a squat team of counter-terrorists took position surrounding the hapless four or five, maybe Bonnie was dazed from her hookah inhalations, Thomas couldn't sort that out yet, he said. Soon enough shots rang out, probably from the squat team, and magically the gunfire ignited the old carriage house which billowed into maximal flames, equal to LeMay's Tokyo festivities of March 9/10, 1945. Against brilliant orange illumination some spectators saw emerging hysterical shrieking figures trying to exit the imminent incineration, but to no avail. Like the hapless Japanese they were vaporized as they strangled for oxygen, and all evidence of previous sexual shenanigans perished, and so the Sears' reputation of luminous strategy seminars endured. Any resonances linking the Hassans to *The Incident* quietly dwelt in the extensive ashes.

Or 2) Dillon managed to get the squat team positioned and there followed three hours of silence before a phone line was established allowing a federal negotiator to initiate discussions first with the Hassans who pled innocent to anything other than enjoying the peculiarities of the Sears' hospitality. In the background the negotiator kept hearing Creighton's moaning about guilt over drowning his daughter and Bonnie's complicity. Eventually Creighton took over the conversation and was persuaded to come out of the carriage house and kneel on the lawn about forty feet in front of the wide doors of that dilapidated building. In sobbing tones he begged the spectators to find the translucent bags holding the two little girls, perhaps in some landfill beyond Fairfax or perhaps in the Atlantic Ocean some miles off the shore. When it seemed that pining wish would be granted, in a rage Nick rushed out of the carriage house and plunged a garden trowel into Creighton's neck killing him instantly and eliciting a hail of gunfire from the squat team. Thereafter in shock and in silent sorrow the Hassans surrendered to be embraced by Ava and Solly.

Or 3) but perhaps you didn't actually want the third and best resolution of America's wondrously atrocious policy. Perhaps you weren't interested in Saif's recitation of America's pillage and slaughter in the history of the world? The incomparable blue spandex oration that so swooned Solly's heart and Thomas's too?

It was clear Thomas was toying with his readers, with his less than excited listener, so it was inevitable to ask which solution he really embraced, and his answer was characteristically coy. He claimed only in the actual writing would he know and reveal how the story ended. He himself couldn't know until he commenced the composition, and that for him was the best part. Not knowing until the writing down revealed it. Until that act, knowing was gloriously inviolate, like history itself. Distraction, as Creighton doubtless came to believe, was all there was, and is.

www.ingramcontent.com/pod-product-compliance
Lightning Source LLC
Chambersburg PA
CBHW070039030726
47506CB00003B/800